Phooey Kerflooey

Kristen Joy Wilks

Copyright © 2024 Kristen Joy Wilks

All rights reserved.

ISBN: **9798879628135**

Scripture quotations are taken from the *Holy Bible*, New Living Translation, copyright ©1996, 2004, 2015 by Tyndale House Foundation. Used by permission of Tyndale House Publishers, Carol Stream, Illinois 60188. All rights reserved.

Cover Design by Lynnette Bonner at Indie Cover Design

Character art by Hayley Kohler at HEKohlerArt

DEDICATION

To Scruffy . . .

First, thank you for having that dream where you babysat while I fought dragons while riding a flying sheep! What woman couldn't dream big after knowing her man dreamed mighty battles for her?

I dreamed of writing a book for years, but it was you who grabbed the flyer for that first writing class and told me, "You should do this!"

I considered the cost of learning the craft. The cost in time, energy, money, and rejection. It was you who said, "But do you love it?"

This one is for you, My Love.

Thank you for washing dishes, wrangling our boys, wiping my tears after rejections, and celebrating acceptance letters. For your love and care every single day and for the madness, mayhem, and fun that you bring into our world. Plus, you were the one to battle squirrels when they rampaged!

I've poured everything I learned from the last twenty-three years of writing into this story but it would never have been written at all if it wasn't for you.

CONTENTS

1	*Daredevils, Squirrel Devils, and Dares*	1
2	*A Quest for Non-Deadly Fun*	8
3	*The Squirrel Declares War*	21
4	*The Puppies Are Mysteriously Massive*	34
5	*Stick to the Plan*	52
6	*Marcus Chooses the Family Moose*	56
7	*Battle Princess, Ragnarök, Dire Bear, or Phooey*	69
8	*Phooey is Afraid*	85
9	*Phooey Needs a Cheering Squad to go Potty*	98
10	*The Squirrel Attacks and Phooey Does Not*	105
11	*Rube Goldberg Machine*	129
12	*Phooey Loves China Teacups More Than Boxing*	141
13	*The Monster's Lair*	165

14	*The Emergency Room Does Not Deal with Squirrels*	179
15	*Squirrel Unleashed*	187
16	*Phooey Smells Danger*	210
17	*Phooey Goes Kerflooey*	221
18	*Phooey's Fearsome "Sit" of Destruction*	232
19	*Puppy Snuggles and an Epic Amount of Cleaning*	246
	Epilogue	260
	Conner's Recipe for Puppy Birthday Cake	271
	Whisper's Story	273
	Acknowledgements	281
	ABOUT THE AUTHOR	285
	Free Stuff!	287

Phooey Kerflooey

CHAPTER ONE
Daredevils, Squirrel Devils, and Dares

Marcus bolted out the door of wheelchair-safe house #4, looking for his little brother, Conner. It had been two seconds. Marcus cleaned his glasses on the edge of his t-shirt and turned in a circle. Where could a ten-year-old in a wheelchair possibly zoom off to in that amount of time?

A squirrel perched on their fence gave an angry chitter. A very familiar squirrel.

"I can't feed you anymore," Marcus said. "No nuts, no bread crusts, no snickerdoodles. Dad and Mom said no. You shouldn't have chewed Dad's work boots."

As the squirrel flicked his tail and darted away, Marcus spotted something fluttering across the decorative rocks that surrounded wheel-chair-safe house #4 instead of grass.

A small piece of paper had settled between the rocks and the rim of the sidewalk. Marcus snatched it up. Maybe Nia had asked Conner to come over to train her guinea pigs to play fetch again.

I see your cast is off. Meet me at the skate park after school. I bet you can't—

Marcus dropped the note without reading the rest and took off.

It didn't matter what Adam Weisburn had bet Marcus's brother. Conner would do it. Conner would rush to do it. Conner would totally battle all of the other kids in their sleepy little town for the right to do it first and fastest, no matter how foolish or dangerous.

Marcus took a right at the library. Maybe he should have gotten Mom or Dad. The skate park was ten whole blocks away.

That was the point of wheelchair-safe house #4. Ten blocks from the skate park (unlike wheelchair-safe house #1), no interior stairs (unlike wheelchair-safe house #3), and no front porch for launching the wheelchair (unlike wheelchair-safe house #2). But Dad hadn't gotten home from work yet and Mom was still on her phone, trying to find out if their rhododendron bush was poisonous.

Why would a young daredevil even want to make his own tea? Conner hated tea. If he'd suddenly decided he needed a hot beverage, why not use a teabag instead of weird leaves he'd found in the yard? He had added a lot of sugar, though.

Marcus pushed himself to run faster. He absolutely could not let his brother get hurt again. Conner had no fear. Marcus needed to have enough fear for both of them.

He'd slept right through Conner tiptoeing outside to go "adventuring" a year before. His little brother had followed an owl, climbed an enormous oak looking for its nest, and slipped on the icy spring branches. The fall had broken his back.

If only Conner had taken Marcus with him . . . Well, Marcus was sticking with his brother now, even if that meant a race to the park when he'd rather be writing or making a boardgame.

Marcus took a left at a small thrift shop called "The Snazzy Goat", then chugged down Maple Street as it angled toward the park. There, at the far end—he could just make out a speeding wheelchair with technicolor lights flashing from both back wheels and a giant squirt gun mounted on the armrest.

Marcus sucked in a deep breath and turned onto the bike path that angled across the park, pushing himself to a full sprint.

Conner was already peering into the giant pit where skateboards and bikes zoomed with pleasant nonchalance, but wheelchairs tended to perform terrifying flips of destruction. He'd just gotten the cast off his leg that proved extreme wheelchair stunts should not be attempted after a mere ten minutes of practice. Both he and Adam Weisburn should know better.

But nope, there was Adam and his new puppy.

Marcus ran a few more steps and then slowed before approaching the boys. He didn't want to startle Conner off the ledge by leaping out of nowhere and seizing his chair. Marcus ducked behind the closest tree. If given the chance, maybe his brother would resist whatever foolishness Adam had in mind.

Adam approached Conner with a sneer on his face that jolted Marcus's heart rate back to super speed. Hadn't one ill-considered dare at the skatepark been enough? The last thing Conner needed was another broken bone.

"Will you do it or are you scared?" Adam shoved his hands in his pockets and smiled.

Conner pulled a spiral flip book out of the storage pocket on the side of his chair and opened it up.

Conner's Shakespearian Insult Generator! The innocent-looking book contained a heap of fancy rudeness from 400 years ago. Hadn't Mom taken that away?

Conner sat tall in his chair and faced his nemesis.

Marcus darted out from behind his tree. "Hi, Adam!" he shouted in a wildly cheerful voice. "Is that a new puppy?"

Conner simply yelled louder, to be heard over Marcus's interruption. "Your wit's as thick as a Tewkesbury mustard."

Adam squinted at the small book, then laughed. "Just 'cause it's Shakespeare doesn't mean it's a good insult."

Dad should never have gotten Conner hooked on Shakespeare. Marcus jogged the last few steps to stand behind his brother and grab his chair. "How about this one," he said, taking a moment to suck in a few breaths of air. "If both of you don't go home now, I'm calling Dad."

"That is a threat, not an insult. You don't even have a phone." Adam knelt and gave his Labrador pup a pat.

"Don't bother Dad, Marcus. I've got this." Conner jerked on his wheels, trying to break Marcus's grip.

"Are you sure, Adam?" Marcus reached into his pocket for the phone he'd made out of cardboard, duct tape, and the ink from three permanent markers. The phone that had been waiting three whole hours for such a time as this.

Adam paused for a long moment, eyeing Marcus. Then he ducked his head and hustled away, the puppy dancing along beside him.

Conner snorted and yanked free. He wheeled back toward the house so fast Marcus had to run to keep up.

Mom met them at the front door. "Honey, did you just make the tea or did you drink any?"

The evil squirrel chittered from his perch on the roof and tossed chewed-up darts down at them.

Mom batted a dart away and gave the boys a stern look.

"I'm fine, Mom. It was just a little tea and my mouth hardly feels funny at all. Why is everyone so boring and—" Conner froze, made a face, then hunched over and vomited into the decorative rocks next to their for-sure-poisonous rhododendron bush.

CHAPTER TWO
A Quest for Non-Deadly Fun

The squirrel was now officially rampaging.

Had the squirrel set out to prove his chaotic prowess before Conner returned from getting his stomach pumped? It was like the wretched rodent heard that Conner was the most destructive living thing in town and had taken offense.

Marcus plopped onto the pebble walkway and sighed, taking in the swath of destruction. Hammocks, ravaged. Homemade comics, mangled. Baseball gloves, nibbled to death. Even their shoelaces were in tatters.

This must be why there were so many "Don't Feed the Wildlife" signs in National Parks. Not for the bears. No, they were worried people would feed the squirrels, encouraging this kind of rampant destruction.

If only they had a dog. A puppy would provide good, wholesome, non-life-threatening fun for his little brother—and chase the squirrel away, too. Marcus could snuggle a dog instead of biting his fingernails in constant terror for his younger sibling. He glanced at the glossy wooden sign Mom had hung over their new back door.

You will keep in perfect peace . . . all whose thoughts are fixed on you. —Isaiah 26:3

Marcus scowled, looking around their dogless, squirrel-ravaged yard. They had a long way to go to perfect anything, much less perfect peace. Perfect chaos, maybe. Conner was bored, Dad and Mom were stressed, even the squirrel seemed unhappy.

They'd lived in all-out pandemonium for so long. What would perfect peace even look like? Marcus pulled in a deep breath and closed his eyes.

The faint warmth of sunshine pressed against his eyelids and a stiff spring breeze brought the scent of grass from other people's yards. Maybe Dad would laugh and make more cheesy puns. Mom wouldn't pace at night or spend so much time searching "How to calm hyper children" on her phone. Conner would find adventure, even in his chair. Marcus would make homemade comics with his brother again. They would finally have their own dog. A dog who would chase away that psycho squirrel.

Perfect peace.

It was pretty much the opposite of a squirrel rampage or a wheelchair flipping end-over-end down concrete steps, wooden steps, brick steps, or a homemade jump. Marcus opened his eyes. There had to be something he could do. Some way to help his parents, calm his brother, chase off the squirrel. A way to get that perfect peace from the sign.

Maybe find something fun for Conner to do? Fun, but not dangerous. A box in the garage caught Marcus's eye: Dad's new bird feeder.

Wildlife was fun. Non-squirrel wildlife. If they couldn't have a puppy, maybe some birds would cheer Conner up. And steer him away from trying to sneak out at night looking for frogs or Sasquatch dens. Marcus pulled a tiny notebook out of his back pocket and bent to snag the pencil he kept tucked beneath the laces of his right shoe.

He scribbled, *Bird Watching*, at the top of the page. Then, *Possible Dangers*. Marcus thought a moment. Conner could flip his chair and Marcus could trip rushing to see some amazing feathered visitor. A bird might steal some of their hair for a nest, or bite them on the finger. He scribbled down these possible perils and then scanned the short list. This was an acceptable level of risk. He drew a smiley face at the top.

Now to make it exciting enough for Conner.

Maybe he could pile adventure upon adventure into a great heap of activity? Like that time Conner had tried to do a wheelie, shoot cans off the fence with his paintball gun, and jump his chair off the porch all at once. Marcus sighed. That had ended their stay in wheelchair-safe house #2, and any hope of having another porch ever again.

Yes, a pile of adventures would do it. Only, safe ones this time.

Marcus hauled the birdfeeder down the twisty little sidewalk that meandered around the house for

Conner's chair and into the front yard. At the center of the decorative rocks there was already a birdbath.

Marcus strung a wire between the house and a fencepost. After filling the feeder with seed, he hung it on the wire, just to the side of the birdbath. The wire sagged in the middle, but at least it held the feeder aloft.

He glanced at the twin windows that looked out into the yard from the front room of the house. Perfect! They could even watch from the safety of the indoors.

That is, if Mom let them into her "showroom" without a hazmat suit. The front room was for clients to see Mom's interior decorator designs. Which was why he and Conner were stuck watching birds instead of roughhousing with their very own puppy. Apparently, none of her designs included dog hair or slobber.

In the next yard over, behind their tall cedar fence, Marcus heard their neighbor, Nia, bouncing on her trampoline. *Sprong, sprong, sprong.* A trampoline wasn't an option for Conner. Marcus froze, imagining Nia sending his brother sky-high with wild bounces.

His pulse sped up. So far Marcus didn't think his brother had his eye on it. Still, Marcus hoped the bird feeder would distract him from joining Nia when he got home from the ER.

Marcus eyed the feeder. "OK, time to add some excitement."

The bouncing behind the fence paused.

Then one more big *sprong* and Nia's fingers appeared at the top of the fence. After a growl and some scuffling, her pink shoe appeared and then her face popped up. "What kind of excitement?"

Nia's brown braids ended in pink sparkle beads today. In fact, her whole face was sparkling.

"You have something on your nose," Marcus said. He squinted as the sunlight glinted off his neighbor's shimmery skin.

"That's glitter lotion and stop changing the subject. You need something exciting for Conner, right?"

"I don't want him to get hurt, but the birdfeeder . . . " Marcus stared at the pleasant but mild feeder. Could they paint some flames on the side or add dramatic music?

"Not really Conner's speed, is it? I'll be right over!" She disappeared.

Marcus heard a few more *sprongs* on the trampoline and then a thump, a crash, and an angry yowl from her cat, Nefurious. He grimaced. Nia was a lot like Conner. Marcus would have to be on high alert, or their "safe but exciting" activity would get his brother injured in no time.

He wandered back to the garage, looking for more ideas. Several cardboard cutouts sat in one corner: a Labrador retriever, a Chihuahua, and a St. Bernard with a lolling tongue. The only dogs Mom allowed.

Marcus set aside the cardboard dogs, then dumped out the box that had their old rollerblades and bug-catching equipment. He spotted their plastic car tracks.

"A Rube Goldberg machine!" Nia shouted from right behind him.

"Gah!" Marcus jumped and caught himself clutching at his chest after Nia's sudden appearance. He took a couple deep breaths while his heart rate slowed. "A what?"

Nia had already darted past and was madly heaping the orange car tracks into her arms.

He straightened his glasses and followed her. "I was thinking maybe a box fort."

"Yes!" She ran out of the garage, leaving a trail of dropped tracks behind her. "A fort plus a Rube Goldberg machine would turn bird watching into a triple-action adventure!"

"What's a Rube Goldberg machine?"

"It's science gone right, that's what! Just watch and learn." She dumped the tracks beside the bird feeder and ran back into the garage. "You guys have little cars, cheese cubes, fishing line, and a bowling ball?"

Marcus ran in and out of the house for supplies while Nia worked. He grabbed an old quilt, four pillows, and two square wicker baskets. He also filled a bag with walnuts, tiny cars, string, a hammer, and tape for Nia. Surely if it was science, no one would get hurt, right?

He hauled everything out to the front yard. A half-dozen birds exited the feeder in a flutter of wings. Awesome! It was already working.

Marcus dragged the box to the edge of the house until the bird feeder was in view. He cut two view ports and a tall, rectangular door with a circle hole for a doorknob. He covered the floor with pillows, spread out the quilt, and attached a wicker basket to the walls by each viewport with zip ties. Despite the hectic morning, a smile relaxed Marcus's face. Their bird-watching fort was going to be awesome.

He filled one wicker basket with pens, lined notebooks, and bags of fishy crackers. He filled the other with pencils, sketchpads, and salty pretzels. A few juice boxes and a plastic jar of chocolate candies, and the whole thing was perfect. He set up the Chihuahua cutout inside the fort and the Labrador retriever and St. Bernard on either side of the cardboard door. They could finally make a new comic together while watching the birds.

Marcus paused to watch Nia build her masterpiece. A masterpiece she had still failed to fully explain. First, she placed a whole walnut on the flat cement at the base of the birdbath. "It's a special treat for any rare birds that show up."

"OK, but that still doesn't tell me what you're building."

"Pure awesomeness!"

Marcus sighed. If Mom and Dad would let him have a phone, he could just look it up. But that wasn't happening until he turned sixteen.

Nia hauled Dad's stepladder up to the house.

"We really shouldn't be on the roof." Marcus started to run inside for his dad, but turned when he heard Nia's footfalls pounding across the shingles. He froze, watching in pure horror. What was she thinking?

Nia made a twisty car track from the ridgeline of the roof all the way down to the edge. She positioned their heaviest car at the top of the track.

A single domino held the car in place. She stuck a string to the bottom of that domino with gum and threaded the string down to Conner's window in their fort.

At the end of the car tracks, above the birdbath, Nia created a web of fishing line. Within that web, she placed the bowling ball. Below the bowling ball, she made a ramp from scraps of an old gutter which she propped up with their tallest stepladder.

Marcus cringed. He had no idea where she'd found the gutter, but she was going to get tetanus for sure! He pounded on the closest window, not willing to take his eyes off Nia. "Dad?" Nothing. Dare he leave her alone to go get help?

Under the wobbly ramp, on the edge of the birdbath, Nia balanced a large metal cooking spoon. She plopped the cubes of cheese into a plastic cup, topped it with foil, and settled the cheese cup into the giant spoon. Then she tethered the spoon to several fenceposts with more fishing line to keep it balanced in place. The handle stuck out, waiting for the bowling ball to flip it into action and send the cheese sailing before the bowling ball proceeded to plumet down upon the hapless walnut below.

"Perfect!" Nia put her hands on her hips and grinned. "You have birdseed for little chickadees, cheese for the crows and grey jays, and then a walnut to crush for your very favorite avian of all! Which is Conner's favorite?"

Marcus stared at her creation. "No, no this is pure insanity, Nia. Someone's going to die by bowling ball!" There were so many ways this could go wrong.

Nia scoffed. "They would have to stand right under the bowling ball ramp. Who in their right mind would do that? Nope, a person sees a bowling ball suspended by fishing line and they say to themselves, 'Welp, better scoot back a bit. That looks very much like a bowling ball all set to crash down in an awesome display of pure science!'"

Marcus gulped. He yanked his notebook from his back pocket and slipped the pencil from under his shoelaces to start scribbling dangers. He ran out of room on the page. There were too many to fathom.

He heard a car pull into the driveway out back. Marcus surveyed their project. His part was ready. The box fort, birdbath, and bird feeder were awesome. The Rube Goldberg machine . . . well, if he got near enough to disengage the madness Nia had set up, that itself would be dangerous. He would tell Mom and Dad right away and then make sure to drive Conner's chair himself so no one got hurt. He took time for three deep breaths. Yeah, despite Nia's foolhardy additions, this was an ideal surprise for a ten-year-old daredevil.

He nodded at the squirrel as he chittered his displeasure. "I'd like to see you ruin that."

"Don't worry," Nia said. "Conner will love it!" Her phone chimed and she scowled. "I gotta go. Tell me how much he loves it, OK?" She sprinted off toward her house.

The squirrel darted away, too. Clearly the critter had nothing to say in the face of their obvious success. Marcus smiled and charged around the house to greet his little brother.

CHAPTER THREE
The Squirrel Declares War

Mom had already parked in the driveway. She sat behind the wheel, staring blankly ahead.

Dad came out of the house and opened the driver's side door for Mom.

Marcus started toward the van but paused when Mom took a breath and smoothed her hands over her face. He wanted to tell her about the dangers of the Rube Goldberg machine, but she looked really stressed.

"I can't believe this happened right before your job interview at Camp Castle Pine," she said. "Can Stella handle them? She's pushing eighty-two and we'll be three hours away. She hasn't run a kid to the ER since you were Conner's age."

Dad pulled Mom into a hug. "Uncle Yule drove until he was a hundred."

Mom didn't look reassured. There might have been tears in her eyes. Marcus looked away and kicked at the driveway with his toe. Job interview, and at a camp? Moving . . . again?

Marcus thought of the only time they'd gone to camp. Horseback rides, shelter-building in rugged swaths of wilderness, plunging through the forest at night to play capture the flag . . . Yeah, a camp was quite possibly the worst location on the planet for his little brother.

Marcus grabbed the remote for Conner's wheelchair lift. If he could make wheelchair-safe house #4 seem fun while still being incredibly safe and calm, maybe Mom and Dad would give up this craziness.

He heaved open the back of the van and scanned his brother for any damage caused by the poisonous tea. Conner looked tired. His red hair stuck up in sweaty spikes and his freckles stood out against skin that was a shade too pale. Still, he grinned when Marcus jammed a button on the remote and the lift began to lower.

"Check this out." Conner waved Mom's phone at Marcus.

Marcus peered at the screen after Conner pushed play. "Gross. What is that?"

"All the guck they pumped out of my stomach. I took the video while Mom was signing papers. Awesome, huh?"

Marcus blinked at the yellow-green sludge. "Well, at least you're not poisoned anymore." Was that frosting and sprinkles in the sludge? "Did you take the last toaster pastry?"

"My stomach hurt."

"That didn't mean you could unlawfully seize my pastry." Marcus released the roll stop and walked beside his brother as he wheeled off the lift and around the van.

Conner did a wheelie, balancing his chair upright for a moment before slamming the wheels back down on the sidewalk. "OK, you can have my next lunchbox treat."

Marcus nodded, accepting his brother's compensation. "Oh, hey. Nia and I made something but we'll have to be really careful." Marcus grabbed the chair's handles and zoomed Conner down the bumpy little sidewalk and around the corner. They lurched to a stop at the edge of the yard. Marcus made a *ta-da* motion toward the fort.

"Oh, yikes!" Conner's eyes widened.

Yikes? That wasn't what he'd been going for. Awesome, hooray, or maybe thank you, but not yikes! Marcus scanned the box fort. Nothing seemed amiss.

Motion on the roof drew his eye. The car from Nia's Rube Goldberg machine came careening down the floppy orange track toward the bowling ball.

The car was not unmanned.

Their evil squirrel crouched on top, his tail streaming out behind.

This wasn't how the Rube Goldberg machine was supposed to be tripped. That infernal rodent had hijacked the grand finale!

The squirrel and barreling car hit the end of the track, bumped the bowling ball, and caused it to thunder down the metal ramp and launch toward the balancing serving spoon. The bowling ball smashed the end of the spoon all right, but that wasn't all it smashed. As the spoon launched the cheese heavenward in a shower of dairy goodness, that bowling ball missed the walnut entirely but hit the base of the birdbath dead on. With its base crushed, the birdbath wobbled for a moment and then tipped. The birdbath cracked in half. The serving spoon kept on soaring straight for Conner who didn't see it because he was ducking pieces of flying cheese. The squirrel leapt. Marcus jumped in front of Conner and batted the kitchen spoon away.

The squirrel landed at the very edge of the broken birdbath.

Marcus couldn't slow down, and tripped on one of the birdbath pieces. He snatched at the squirrel as he fell, smacking the birdbath's rim. His fingers flashed with pain as the largest piece of birdbath flipped, launching the squirrel.

Marcus crashed into the rocks, mashing his shoulder and leg.

The birdbath came down a moment later, crunching right on top of his toe.

The squirrel landed like a superhero who'd just leapt a tall building. He darted up the side of the house and sprang onto the drooping bird feeder.

The feeder swung, the wire sagged further, and finally the whole thing snapped. The squirrel rode the falling bird feeder down like a tiny cowboy. The feeder and squirrel smashed on top of the broken birdbath. The feeder exploded.

Seeds scattered everywhere but the squirrel remained calm. He sat on top of the carnage, flicked an arrogant tail, and nibbled delicately at a fool's fortune in bird seed.

"Oh, wow!" Conner said. But his voice did not ring with joy or the anticipation of many relaxing hours spent watching birds. It sounded pretty much the same as Marcus's when he'd seen Conner's video of the vomit.

Only two things remained unscathed: the box fort and the walnut. Well, three if you counted the squirrel. The gluttonous creature continued to chow down.

Marcus dragged himself upright. He limped forward, waving his arms at the squirrel.

Phooey Kerflooey

Conner yanked off one shoe and flung it. "Ye veriest varlet that ever chewed with a tooth!"

Marcus gave a sad laugh. At least Conner was making better use of the Shakespearian Insult Generator.

The squirrel glanced up, blinked, and flicked his tail in disdain. He didn't move from his pirated hoard.

Marcus made another move toward the squirrel. The unvexed creature leapt off the broken feeder in a graceful arch. He grabbed the unbroken walnut, then scampered across the rocks and skittered up the side of the house with squirrely aptitude.

Dad walked up behind them. "So, that's what Rasputin's been up to."

"Rasputin?" Marcus asked.

"I named him after a Russian mystic from over a hundred years ago who was really hard to get rid of," Dad said. "Some accounts say he was poisoned, shot, and drowned."

"Like me!" Conner raised both hands in victory.

"No," Dad said. "You were only poisoned and that caused enough trouble. Marcus, let me know if

27

Conner goes anywhere near a cannon or large puddle of water?"

Marcus nodded, even though he spotted Dad's smile. Dad wasn't really worried, but maybe he should have been.

"We do need to get rid of Rasputin, though," Dad said. He glanced at the destruction in the yard, then at their fort, peering closer at the cardboard dogs.

Marcus crawled inside the box fort to see if Rasputin had caused any damage. Sure enough, Rasputin had clearly been there. There were holes chewed in the pillows and right through the side of their box. Their snacks were scattered. Every single package of cheesy fish and pretzels had been nibbled. Every single one. Marcus started picking them up, then froze. Conner's sketch pad was covered in stinky brown pellets and Marcus's big story notebook had bite marks on the cover.

How could they find any kind of peace with Rasputin rampaging every time they tried to do something outside?

He dropped the holey snack packets and crawled out. Conner had wheeled off to look for another box and Dad was still standing in the same spot, the cardboard Chihuahua in his hands.

Marcus yanked his tiny notebook out of his back pocket and grabbed his pencil. He wrote: *Perils of Building a New Box Fort: 1) Falling birdbath.* That had already fallen. *2) Falling bird feeder.* Been there, done that. *3) Falling trees.* They didn't have any trees.

Well, it was safe enough. He stuffed the pencil back under his shoelaces.

A piercing scream came from the other side of the house.

Dad took off, Marcus right behind him. They rounded the corner just as Conner barreled past in his chair. Marcus spotted Mom slumped against the back wall of the garage. Her face was pale and she had one hand pressed against her throat. Marcus looked around. There wasn't anything dangerous—just Rasputin, darting away.

She turned toward Dad. "Will the insurance cover squirrel damage?" When Dad only grimaced, she whispered, "Look," and opened one of the heavy plastic tubs that held her interior design stuff. A squirrel-sized hole had been chewed in the lid.

Marcus crept closer and surveyed the damage. Wallpaper samples had been shredded to make a huge nest smack in the middle of some fancy leather pillows. Mom knelt by the tub and pulled one out from under the nest. "I was supposed to match these for a client." Her voice cracked. "They come from her $6,000 couch."

Mom's eyes narrowed. "Thankfully, that squirrel didn't get into this one." She opened a tub with a bolt of shiny fabric. "Silk velvet drapery," she whispered. "$199.95 a yard." Her face went from pale to red alarmingly fast. "We've got to do something. I can't do business like this."

A heavy silence filled the garage as Mom glanced between the destroyed pillows and the super-fancy fabric.

"My paintball gun!" Conner shouted. He spun his chair and wheeled to the other side of the garage where his gear was stowed. "That bolting-hutch of beastliness!" Conner stared into his box. "A whole bag of paintballs is gone and the hopper has a hole chewed in it."

Marcus looked between Mom and Conner. Mom's hands trembled. Conner's fists clenched.

Marcus turned to his dad.

Dad tapped one finger calmly against the cardboard cutout of the Chihuahua. "Can you boys get lunch while I help your mother clean up?"

Conner seemed too distracted to help, so Marcus went by himself into the kitchen. Maybe ramen noodles and scrambled egg sandwiches would help? He heated the water, broke a few eggs, and got some butter sizzling in the pan.

Dad walked through the garage door with the nest of wallpaper samples and Mom followed with the chewed-up pillows. She paused a moment and then mashed them into the trash.

When Mom spotted a stack of puppy research papers on the counter that Marcus had rescued from the recycle bin, she released a long, slow breath. "Honey, I already told you. With all the messes dogs make, we absolutely cannot have—" She paused, then picked up the printout on top. "Scottish terriers are known for chasing away rodents," she mumbled. "Rats, mice, moles, and squirrels should steer clear of even the meekest Scottie." Mom glanced at Dad as he struggled to cram all the shredded wallpaper into the trash.

A crash from the front yard rattled the windows. Marcus ran to look.

Conner had made a wheelchair jump with a couple of boards from the garage and the broken birdbath. His chair was upside-down, one wheel spinning lazily. Conner sprawled on the rocks beneath the successfully launched wheelchair.

Mom gasped and pressed against the window.

"I'm fine, Mom," Conner shouted. "No worries." He gave them a thumbs up.

Dad charged outside to pull Conner upright and dust him off.

Marcus picked up one of his favorite puppy pages and slipped it into Mom's hands.

She met his gaze and then slowly glanced at the paper. "Newfoundlands are known for being excellent therapy dogs. Their tranquil demeanor and soothing presence is perfect for bringing joy to hurting individuals in a hospital setting, encouraging the elderly in nursing homes, or even calming rowdy children in the classroom."

Dad walked in, still holding the cardboard Chihuahua. "Honey, have you ever thought that maybe . . . " Dad lifted the Chihuahua cutout and made it prance along the counter. He gave its cardboard tail a wag and raised one eyebrow at Mom.

Mom glanced at Dad, then back at the puppy research pages. "Marcus, where was your list of local litters? I don't believe I paid your suggestion the attention it deserved."

CHAPTER FOUR
The Puppies Are Mysteriously Massive

The family van rattled down a gravel road toward the paintball field. Aunt Stella clutched the wheel tight. Every time they encountered a pothole, she gasped out, "Gracious gophers!" Aunt Stella looked especially colorful today in her green scarf, flowery skirt, and the neon guinea pig socks Nia had given her peeking through her usual Birkenstocks. "They won't actually shoot the paintballs at each other, will they, dear? It's practice, after all."

"Of course, they do," Conner yelled from the back. "That's the fun of it. You wanna be on my team or Nia's?"

"Oh, no." Aunt Stella shook her head, some of her wispy hair escaping its hasty ponytail. "We've got to go get that puppy." She slowed the van to a crawl and oozed over a cattle guard at the speed of a nearly unconscious snail.

Marcus allowed himself a small smile. Since Dad and Mom had left for the job interview, he'd been given the solemn duty of choosing their puppy.

An actual living, breathing, barking puppy. Not a papier-mâché, robotic, or cardboard canine, but a warm puffball full of wiggles and wags and doggy smiles. Real fur. Real puppy kisses. Real doggy breath. All they had to do was drop off Conner at paintball practice, then Marcus and Aunt Stella would pick up their new dog.

Marcus had researched how to choose the perfect pup from a litter, made a chart of puppy characteristics to look for, and had even practiced by observing Nia's cat and guinea pigs. Nonetheless, his heart still pounded too loud in his ears. It wasn't even because Conner had told him to choose the pup "most likely to battle a rhinoceros."

Mom had said yes to a squirrel-chasing, Conner-soothing dog . . . but she had also made some additional demands.

The dog had to be small, easy to brush, and retreat to the linoleum on command when clients were over. The pup should not slobber, shed on clothes or furniture, or eat expensive kibble. And their new canine companion must be both comforting for Conner and bold enough to chase away that evil squirrel.

A Scottish terrier would be perfect. Marcus sucked in a deep breath. He had nothing to worry about. Scotties were known for chasing rodents and required minimal brushing. Staying on the linoleum would come with training.

Marcus shifted in his seat. Another pothole toppled a pile of library books on dog care and dumped his puppy folder full of computer printouts that featured every single available pup within 100 miles. He probably didn't need it anymore, now that Mom had chosen a litter. Marcus smiled and picked up the folder he did need. This one only had papers about their chosen breed, the fun and fearless Scottish terrier!

Once Rasputin had sent Mom into a puppy-finding fury, she'd simply perused Marcus's research and chosen an appropriate kind of dog for their family. The adorable pictures and pages full of informative text from the American Kennel Club represented hours of research, but it had worked. Mom had already paid for their pup online.

Marcus felt a little dizzy and realized that he was holding his breath and squeezing the puppy folder in a white-knuckled grip. Relax, he commanded himself. Everything would be fine. He just had to pick the right puppy for both Conner and Mom.

The van lurched to a stop in front of a grass field full of inflatable paintball bunkers. Aunt Stella peered at the dash, poking buttons until she finally turned the headlights off.

Marcus pulled the tiny notebook out of his pocket and tugged the pencil out from under his laces. He wrote: *Choosing a Puppy:* What is the worst thing that could happen? *1) There are no puppies left. 2) All the puppies are rabid. 3) Mom accidentally bought a llama. 4) None of the puppies like me.* Marcus scanned the list. None of these hazards seemed likely. No, this was a safe activity, even for a twelve-year-old. He could do this.

"Good gravy, what's that button for?" Aunt Stella sat in the driver's seat, waving Conner's wheelchair lift remote toward the back of the van and pushing random buttons. Aunt Stella was actually their great-great-aunt and older than Grandma. Both the wheelchair lift and finding the shopping channel easily stumped her.

Conner reached over the back seat and held out a hand. "Just give it to me. I'm gonna be late." Aunt Stella peered at the small device and mashed another button. Conner bumped his chair against the roll stop. "This is taking forever."

Marcus scrambled for the spare remote before his brother could get impatient and launch himself over the roll stop—again.

After Marcus got his brother's lift going, Conner grabbed his paintball marker, mask, and a granola bar from a row of handy seat pockets. He dropped the bar and grimaced. "Nasty! Rasputin got into the snacks. Better check on your game, Marcus."

His brother was right. Marcus reached into the highest pocket and removed the box that held "Puppy Panic," the game he'd made so he and Conner could practice their dog-ownership skills. Brown pellets tumbled out and the top card showed signs of chewing. It was one he'd made as a joke. The card read, "Your puppy is super proud and cannot walk upon the soil like a mere dog. Make a path of potholders, mittens, and winter hats so that he can safely travel to the water bowl."

Marcus tossed the damaged card in the trash. It was one of Conner's favorites, too. Of course, they still had the Hail of Hotdogs card: "Your puppy gets loose in the meat section of the grocery store and rampages. Lose one obedience point chasing him down and paying for the damage." He'd have to wipe all the cards down before they played again. Although, he wasn't sure the card game had improved their dog-ownership skills. They'd never gotten their pups through more than five turns. One of them always drew a Startled Skunk card or Plague of Stray Cats and lost all their obedience points.

Conner shouted out a few final suggestions as he grabbed a water bottle and checked his gear. "Get the biggest, craziest puppy they have. I'm so sick of that squirrel!"

Marcus nodded. Rasputin was a pain. Marcus wasn't sure how Conner expected him to check the puppies for squirrel-chasing skills, though.

Conner slammed his mask into place and grinned. "Do you want to borrow my backup marker and a handful of paintballs? If you shot off a few rounds near the puppies, you could pick out the bravest one, easy."

Marcus grimaced. "Don't worry, I have a plan. I'll bring back just the right pup." The library books said to sit quietly in a corner and observe the puppies. Nowhere did it say to test their speed, wrestling ability, or whether or not they might be capable of mutating into something that belonged in an old monster movie.

Phooey Kerflooey

Conner had high hopes for their new dog. So did Mom. What she wanted and what Conner wanted, though . . .

Well, an eagerness to attack bears wasn't high on Mom's list.

Aunt Stella came around the van to the lift door as Conner wheeled onto the field, paintball marker already slotted onto the swivel holder that Marcus had mounted on the side of his chair. "He's already gone? I just got my seatbelt off." She watched Conner spin out on the wet grass, park behind one of the blow-up bunkers, and then test his marker by spraying the nearby forest with a hail of paintballs.

"Do the other children watch out for him? Because of his chair, I mean?"

Marcus laughed, making Aunt Stella raise her eyebrows. "Not anymore."

Marcus and Aunt Stella watched Conner wheel his chair hard with one hand, sending it into a diagonal lurch as he aimed his marker at Nia. "Eat paint you flap-eared knave!"

Nia put her hands on her hips. "Hey, they haven't even blown the—"

Conner pulled the trigger in rapid succession.

Nia spluttered as paint sprayed her mask. "Argh, you little twerp!" Apparently, paint had gone through the plastic grill and into her mouth, because Marcus could hear her spitting and gagging all the way across the field. Instead of raising her marker over her head in acknowledgement of the hit, Nia let out a feral growl and flung her marker away. With a clatter of beaded braids, she bowled Conner over in a flying tackle, chair and all.

The referee screamed as the wheelchair slid backwards down the hill with Nia sitting on Conner's chest, whacking him over the head with her pink-camouflaged shoe while he grinned.

Yeah, Conner couldn't resist showing off for Nia.

Aunt Stella gasped. "Oh, my! Do you think we should—"

"Drive?" Marcus interrupted, opening the driver's side door for his aunt. "Absolutely! The puppies won't wait forever. Conner's having a blast."

And he was. Marcus shook his head as he watched his little brother laughing while the ref tried to pry Nia away long enough to right the chair.

"Ah, yes. Well I suppose . . . " She shook her head and turned away from the ruckus, patting her pockets for the keys.

Yeah, the other kids had quit taking it easy on Conner pretty quick. His bursts of arrogant bragging, coupled with a talent for memorizing and using Shakespearian insults, had ended that. Now, not only did the other kids treat him like everyone else, they went after Conner with special relish.

Marcus's little brother got shot an awful lot, but Conner also managed to squeeze in his fair share of hits. There was a reason they hadn't kicked him off the team. Sometimes Conner was almost too infuriating to bear, but he was a talented and driven athlete even without the use of his legs.

Marcus sighed. A puppy would help. He'd read how universities were bringing in puppies to calm stressed-out college kids during big tests and about therapy dogs helping kids learn to read. A new puppy would bring some peace and quiet into their lives. Conner would settle down a little and Mom and Dad wouldn't worry so much. Especially when their pup chased away Rasputin. They needed to get their furry canine home and into Conner's arms immediately.

Aunt Stella leaned against the van before getting back inside, puffing to catch her breath. "Your mom said he needed special care. She never said anything about me needing special care after trying to keep up with him." Aunt Stella laughed as though she'd made a joke. Marcus didn't join her.

It would not be funny if this puppy thing didn't work. Conner was indeed hard to keep up with. Dad was tired. Mom was tired. Could Aunt Stella actually be tired after only two hours? Marcus had woken up at 1:00 this morning when he caught Conner sneaking out again with his bug-catching equipment for some "adventuring." Marcus had been vigilant all year, trying to keep Conner out of mischief, but he was exhausted. Something had to change or Marcus might never sleep again.

"I read an article that said a puppy can help kids be less restless and hyper," Marcus told Aunt Stella. "With a puppy to snuggle, he'll want to read books, do art projects, and start baking again."

Aunt Stella met his gaze for a long moment, then nodded.

This was a good idea, right? A horrible thought flitted through his mind. What if adding a small furry animal to their home didn't bring a soothing calm, after all?

Rasputin was small and furry and all he brought was destruction and poo pellets.

No, the research was solid. The presence of a pet decreased stress, taught empathy, responsibility, and self-control. A pet could even help heal PTSD. A puppy would make everything easier. "Puppy" and "Peace" even started with the same letter!

Puppy ownership would most definitely send Conner into a baking and drawing frenzy—a calm frenzy, of course.

"Did you know we used to make our own comics?" Marcus said. "Conner would draw the craziest pictures and I would make a story from them."

Aunt Stella nodded, but looked unconvinced. Marcus didn't blame her. Conner hadn't illustrated a story since his accident. Only the most ill-considered activities seemed to please him now.

Aunt Stella climbed back in the van and struggled to buckle up. She read Mom's note stuck to the navigation system: "Press here to find puppies." She poked the button and gasped when a calm British voice ordered her to travel twelve feet and then turn right. Aunt Stella glanced over her shoulder. "Next stop, puppies!"

They followed a small country highway for about thirty minutes before turning down a winding dirt road with a stripe of grass growing down the center.

Marcus took a deep breath as they neared their goal. Since it was spring break on Monday, the boys would have a whole week with their pup before they had to go back to school. The breeder was chosen, the litter was ready, Conner's latest cast was finally off, and the puppy was paid for. He could do this.

Marcus opened his folder to read up on Scottish terriers one more time. He sorted the info into stacks.

One pile for temperament. "The Newfoundland is gentle and calm, wonderful with children and a true soothing influence." Hmmm, Mom had left some papers from the general puppy folder in with all the info about Scottish terriers. All the dogs had black fur, but some were a whole lot bigger than a Scottie.

One pile for training. "Newfoundlands are eager to learn and easy to train." Marcus blinked. These puppies were definitely not Scottish terriers.

One pile for size and grooming needs. "Scotties only need to be groomed once a month and reach a maximum size of twenty-two pounds." He peered closer. These puppies were black, like the Newfoundlands, and had small triangle ears that pricked up partway, like the wings of an airplane. Newfoundlands had droopy ears. The pups on this page had wiry coats and shorter tails, too. These were definitely the right puppies.

He glanced over the other papers. The temperament stack showed a large black dog with a long sweeping tail, floppy triangular ears, and a soft looking coat. Was Mom expecting a dog with the personality of the Newfoundland, but the size of a

Scottie? No, she'd seen all his research. He was worrying over nothing.

Aunt Stella pulled up to an old wooden barn near a field of clover. A weathered sign swung from the thick branch of a maple that hung out over the road. It read "Shady Puddle Farm" in faded lettering. A white farmhouse with a porch swing and huge front windows sat nearby.

A dark, shaggy shape lumbered across the field between the house and the barn. Whatever it was, the creature was massive. It disappeared behind the barn before Marcus could get a good look. Did they have black bears out here? A woman in jeans and a flannel shirt burst through the front door, letting the screen slam behind her.

"You must be Stella," she shouted. When Aunt Stella opened the car door, the woman snatched up her hand, pumping her arm in an enthusiastic handshake. She gave Marcus a wave and then half-dragged his aunt toward the barn.

Marcus followed behind, tucking his papers back into the puppy folder.

"Here are the new babies." The flannel lady opened the top half of a stall door. The space was full of straw and a swarm of black puppies. When the woman leaned toward them, all the puppies bounded over in a wave of wagging tails. They put their paws up on the side and yipped and wagged and nibbled at her long braid as it hung over the half-door. The biggest black pup rolled over, begging for belly rubs.

Marcus stopped. These had to be adult dogs. He looked at the size and grooming page in the puppy folder. A Scottie pup was supposed to weigh four to five pounds at eight weeks. They reached twenty-two pounds at adulthood. These puppies were far too big and much fuzzier than expected.

"How much do they weigh?" Marcus asked, wondering why she had crammed ten adult Scotties into a single stall.

The flannel woman beamed at him. "I just weighed them yesterday and our largest pup is a whopping twenty-two pounds."

He smiled back, but a strange cold crept through him and his stomach did a sick flop. "So, where are the puppies?" he asked, his mind refusing to accept what his eyes saw.

The animals in the stall certainly acted like puppies, tripping all over each other, galloping in wild circles, falling asleep almost instantly when Marcus didn't approach the gate. They formed a furry pile of big paws and wet noses that made him want to stroke their soft fur and forget about the size discrepancy.

"Did you want to meet the parents?" The woman marched over to a side door and gave a long whistle.

Marcus heard a thumping sound coming toward them, and fast. Had the flannel lady accidentally caught the attention of a herd of bison or maybe some wild pigs? Marcus took a step back, certain that a galloping brachiosaurus was about to enter the old barn.

The door burst open and the lady waved her arms. "Sit!"

Two huge dogs skidded to a stop, plopping their big furry bottoms down in the straw. Slobber dripped from their open mouths as they panted, large pink tongues lolling in doggy grins. Long, silky tails wagged, thumping against the side of the barn and sending straw flying. They had soft-looking black fur, droopy triangle ears, and dark happy eyes. The giant dogs were most definitely Newfoundlands, not Scottish terriers.

"How much do they weigh?" Marcus whispered.

"Oh goodness, let's see. Nana weighs 140 pounds and Reuben here is about 160. He's a little larger than average, but he's a bit taller than normal, too. The vet says he's healthy as a bear, though."

"Did you say 160 pounds?"

The flannel lady nodded enthusiastically.

"Just, um, could you give me a minute?"

CHAPTER FIVE
Stick to the Plan

The flannel lady smiled and tugged his aunt over to look at her dog show trophies. Marcus borrowed Aunt Stella's ancient phone and rushed outside. Reuben weighed 160 pounds! He was double Marcus's weight. Marcus gulped. That dog was bigger than Mom.

He glanced down at the phone, ready to text. It was the kind you had to flip open, with teeny tiny buttons too small for his fingers. He gave up and dialed Mom's number, even though she'd written "For Emergencies Only" on the 3x5 card. How would they even walk a dog that huge?

"Hi there, Stella," his mom answered. "What's up?"

"It's me. The puppies weigh like twenty-two pounds already!"

"Marcus? Is that you? The connection is a bit scratchy. Can you say that again?"

"The puppies weigh twenty-two pounds and they're only eight weeks old." He talked loud and slow, hoping Mom would hear. "That's eighteen pounds more puppy."

"That's the size I was expecting, but it will take a year or so for them to grow up."

"No, they're that size now!" he shouted. The phone cut out again.

"Of course, you'll want to see some adults, too. That's not a problem. I'm not sure what you're worried about."

"The puppies are the size of an adult and the adult is the size of a moose!"

"Oh, you got to see a moose. How exciting, I didn't realize the breeder lived that far out in the country. Try to get a picture if you see it again, OK?"

"Not a moose, a dog. The dog was as big as a moose!"

The line crackled and Marcus listened hard, hoping to catch a few of his mom's words. The static cleared just long enough for him to make out her next sentence. "If you make a good plan and stick to it, everything will turn out fine. Dad and I will see you Wednesday evening, all right?"

Marcus was pretty sure the plan was already shot, but he tried one more time. "Should I get the puppy? They don't look like we expected. They're huge, like big furry bears."

"Oh my goodness, you saw a bear and a moose!" More static. "What a day, Sweetie. I'm so glad that Aunt Stella was able to drive you out right at the perfect time to see so much wildlife."

"What about the puppies? They are super-big."

"Yes, get the puppy. Conner will love a super one. I know you can do this. The decision will be good for you." He tried to interrupt while the call was free of static, but Mom just kept rambling. "You know how much Conner could use a distraction right now. Pick a friendly pup who needs two boys and lots of snuggles. I've got to go, Sweetie. The camp director is giving us a tour. They have rustic wheelchair ramps across the entire campus now." His mom hung up.

He swallowed hard. Conner shouldn't live at a camp way out in the woods. It would just remind him of everything he couldn't do.

Marcus stood frozen for a moment. Maybe he could text after all. He mashed out a message on the tiny buttons. After several minutes, he'd managed to type out: *Puppies twenty-two pounds right now and—* then the phone shut off. Oh, no, the battery! He'd seen Aunt Stella's charger on the counter before they'd left.

Marcus stared into the field where the biggest of the monstrous dogs had decided to stop, drop, and roll right in the center of a mud puddle. What was he supposed to do now?

CHAPTER SIX
Marcus Chooses the Family Moose

Marcus held the dead phone in his hand, listening to the silence.

Slowly, he became aware of sounds around him. The chatter of chickadees in the old oak tree. The scratching of the chickens as they clawed the dirt, looking for bugs. The rush of wind tearing through the bright spring grasses that grew tall underneath the split-rail fence lining the driveway.

Mom wanted him to bring home a puppy, but she didn't understand there'd been a mistake.

"Come on, God," he whispered. Less a prayer and more like filling out an official complaint form at the school office. "We prayed about this, asked what we should do to help Conner. Then boom, Mom finally listened to my puppy idea. Wasn't that You?"

A new sound broke the stillness of the sunny afternoon. *Thump, thump, kalump, thump, thump, kalump.*

He looked up and scrambled to get behind the oak tree.

A bear lurched to a stop and sat right in front of him, its tongue lolling out the side of its mouth and its tail wagging.

Oh, not a bear. The momma dog, Nana. Where had the muddy one gone? Marcus looked up and down the narrow country road, hoping to spot him before getting smeared with mud and/or slobber.

Nana thumped her tail again and then nosed his hand.

Marcus reached out slowly.

She sighed and gazed at him with gentle brown eyes as if to say, "Well, are you going to pet me or not? I don't have all day."

He rested his hand on the huge dog's head.

She leaned against his leg with a contented groan.

Marcus scratched her ears and smoothed his hand down her massive back. Her fur was incredibly soft, like the plush velvet blankets and throw pillows Mom used in her showroom.

What if he did like Mom said and brought home a puppy?

He pulled out his notebook and slid the stub of pencil from underneath his shoelaces. Marcus wrote: *Risks of Getting a Newfoundland Puppy: 1) Cuteness overload.* A real risk. *2) Too large.* But Mom did say yes. *3) Too furry.* But Mom did say yes. *4) Too slobbery.* But Mom did say yes. *5) Too perfect for Conner.* Not a problem.

Sure, Nana was the size of a small bear, but Conner had talked about getting a dog large enough to pull his wheelchair like it was an ancient Roman chariot. He would love a big dog, even if chariot racing was off-limits. Nana was gentle and soft and loving. All the things his mom had wanted. One of these pups would be just as fun as a Scottish terrier. It could snuggle while they read books and keep Conner from breaking more bones in ill-considered dares. A big pup would chase Rasputin away from their shoelaces and play fetch exactly like a small pup. A huge dog could soothe his brother's restlessness and be just as good a friend as a small dog.

Nana nudged him with her snout when he stopped petting.

Marcus scratched her ear, his mind a whirl of possibilities.

What was wrong with these puppies?

Nothing.

There was nothing wrong with these puppies! He'd even double checked with Mom and she'd pretty much ordered him to choose a puppy and bring it home.

Marcus gave Nana one more pat and took off toward the barn. His brother needed a puppy. Their whole family needed a dog and Marcus was going to make sure that they had one. Just the right one.

The perfect puppy.

"Oh, there you are, Marcus." Aunt Stella was bent over the stall door talking to the puppies and defending her green scarf from their sharp teeth. "Just look at these little guys. Have you ever seen anything more adorable in your life?"

Marcus leaned over the half-door and grinned. Ten black furballs tumbled and tripped all over each other, fighting to be the first to lick his hand. They were super-cute. "Which one is the smallest pup?" he asked the flannel lady.

She squinted at the pups. After a moment she pointed to a huge puppy who was pushing an empty food dish around looking for more tidbits. "Daisy there. She only weighs eighteen pounds, but with the way she's going after her food, I don't think she'll stay small for long."

Hmmm . . . none of the puppies were small, not really. Maybe he needed a new plan. Getting the smallest pup probably wouldn't make a difference to Mom. They were all huge. But what about a sweet girl puppy? Like a little sister, only fuzzier.

To make Conner happy, he would get either a really fierce girl pup or a really big one.

It was perfect.

"How many girl puppies are there?" Three pups fought over who would get to nibble on his fingers.

"You're in luck. The litter before this one only had one girl. This time around I have six girls and four boys, but let me check with my daughter. She's choosing one of the girls to keep." The flannel lady opened the stall door and waded into the puppies, her hands full with a fresh dish of food.

The puppies went berserk, yipping and bouncing all over the place, their little black tails windmilling.

She set the dish down and the pups dove in.

The flannel lady stepped out of the swarm of puppies and shut the stall door. "Why don't you sneak on in and sit in the corner. See which puppies come over to say hi. I'll go get Jessie and find out which one she's settled on."

Marcus slowly creaked the door open and slipped into the stall. He tiptoed over to the far corner, prepared to sit on a mound of straw and watch each puppy to figure out its personality.

He was *not* prepared for what actually happened.

The straw crackled as he sat. The puppies' heads popped up at the sound. Wet dog food clung to their furry muzzles. Even their ears were soggy with supper. Ten black tails wagged wildly. Twenty bright eyes met his gaze. Forty furry paws launched into action.

The puppies charged.

They galloped across the stall, floppy ears flapping, droopy tails thrashing, and grubby little snouts letting out a chorus of yips and barks.

Marcus held his hands in front of his face to protect himself as he was bowled over by all ten puppies at once.

They attacked in a flurry of slurps, washing his ears and chin and eyes. Slobber, soggy puppy chow, and fur flew everywhere. When he tried to open his mouth, puppies slurped there too. He gagged and struggled to free himself from the avalanche of cuteness.

A strong hand yanked him to his feet and a little girl's laughter rose above the yips and yaps. "Better not take all ten. I don't think you could handle it."

"Are you OK?" the flannel lady asked.

Marcus nodded and dug around in the straw for his glasses. He turned to the girl. "I had no intention of taking all ten." He brushed straw off his pants and wiped the slobber from his lenses before putting them back on to give the girl a glare.

"There's still some in your hair, and on your shirt, and did you look at your socks?"

After brushing himself off again and wiping a string of slobber from his cheek, Marcus met her gaze. "Better?"

"Much. Now, Mom is going to feed the goats so I'll help you choose a pup. Did you want a male or a female?"

Would having a girl puppy be anything like trying to talk to Jessie, the bossy puppy expert? Marcus wondered if he should reconsider and look at one of the male pups. No, he needed something for everyone. Dad would like whichever they picked, but both Mom and Conner needed just the right pup. A girl for Mom and the largest puppy for Conner . . . or should he get the fiercest?

"Which puppy is the fiercest? My little brother kind of wanted a guard dog, but my mom wants a dog with a soothing temperament."

Jessie huffed out a breath and gave him an annoyed look. "Newfoundlands are not known for being good guard dogs. Dice, here," she picked up a chubby black pup with white markings, "is the fiercest as far as fighting his way to the food dish, but he is also the laziest. He sleeps all day, waiting for the next meal to arrive. So, do you want a fierce dog or do you want a soothing dog?"

Marcus stuffed down an angry response and considered the question. So, a guard dog wasn't an option. That made it easy. A girl puppy for Mom and the biggest pup for Conner. That should please the whole family.

"OK, which is the biggest girl puppy?"

With a soft smile, Jessie pointed to a roly-poly pup who was curled into a ball in the corner of the stall snoring softly. "I thought about keeping this little fuzzball myself. She's the largest, but is completely terrified of fingernail polish."

"You painted the puppies' toenails? That's horrible."

"No, it's not. Sometimes a girl wants to look her best." Jessie stood and all the puppies scattered, including the biggest, who sprang out of her nap and into a rowdy gallop. Jessie chased the puppies around for a minute. Finally, she struggled back to Marcus with her arms full of the very large pup.

"This one is a big, beautiful princess. She's twenty-two pounds, one of the biggest pups we've ever had and has already been registered as 'Shady Puddle's Princess Foo Foo Bear'."

"Oh, wow. You named her after foo dogs, like those fierce stone statues of Chinese lions that guard palaces and stuff?"

"Nope. 'Foo Foo,' as in a teeny-weeny little dog that rides in a purse, wears a barrette in her hair, and gets carried on all her walks so she doesn't get dirty. Hilarious, huh? Can you imagine this big girl in a purse?" She patted the puppy's head and pulled some bow-shaped clips from her pocket to fasten above the puppy's floppy ear. "She does like to be pampered, though. Don't you, girl." Jessie employed a nauseating baby voice that could totally belong to the owner of an actual foo-foo dog. Princess Foo Foo Bear seemed to appreciate the attention. She held perfectly still until Jessie snapped the last bow.

Phooey Kerflooey

Wow, this was going to go over real well with Conner. Marcus couldn't have thought of a less-brave name if he'd tried. "That's just her registered name, right? We can change it or call her something else." Marcus met her glare with one of his own, daring her to say different.

"I suppose, but I've been calling her Princess Foo Foo Bear all week. Sometimes, when she gets into trouble, I'll call her Phooey Kerflooey, but I usually just use her registered name. She comes to Princess Foo Foo Bear and everything. It'd be a pain to start training her over again." Jessie plopped down in the corner and patted the straw beside her. Marcus sat and leaned closer to examine the pup.

The puppy was certainly big. Her paws looked like they should belong to a little bear and her head was huge. He patted his lap and the puppy tumbled over. She climbed onto his legs. "Sit!" he told her. Instead, she jumped up and put both front paws on his chest in order to give his face a big lick. Oh yeah, this puppy was great. Conner would be thrilled, and Mom—well, this was a little-girl dog. Mom would love to have another girl around the house.

"Here, you'll need her ear bows and especially her doll baby." Jessie held out a little backpack with dog paws on it. "Her blanky is also in there. It helps to have something that smells like her momma and littermates for her first few nights."

"Oh, I don't think we need ear bows or a doll. We'll get her some toys at home."

"She likes these. If she's holding her ballerina doll, she's even brave enough to chase birds. She needs this stuff. Sometimes things scare puppies and they want something that smells like home." She pushed the backpack into Marcus's arms. He saw there was a small bag of puppy chow inside, as well as a leash and brush.

"OK. I want her to feel at home. Have you tried calling her Princess Attack Bear?"

Jessie huffed and rolled her eyes.

The flannel lady hustled back and went over first-night care with Aunt Stella. Jessie droned on and on about all of Princess Foo Foo Bear's—no, he would not even think that name—about *the puppy's* favorite musical numbers. According to Jessie, this pup leaned toward soundtracks from princess movies, especially those with singing furniture or forest animals that danced.

Marcus clipped the leash to the pup's collar. The puppy sat and stared up at him, her tail thumping when he bent to stroke her soft fur.

Yeah, he'd made the right choice. She was big and fluffy and awesome. This puppy was exactly what their family needed.

Having a puppy would make everything better.

CHAPTER SEVEN
Battle Princess, Ragnarök, Dire Bear, or Phooey

When they picked up Conner from paintball practice, Marcus made a spot on the bench seat and tried to help him into the van.

Conner glared and brushed him away. "Just boost me to the handhold."

Marcus sighed, but did so. His brother's way took longer and had to be exhausting, but Conner had been a monkey-bar fanatic in kindergarten, so Marcus supposed it made sense.

Instead of more help, Conner used a series of sturdy loops Dad had bolted to the van to get inside. Usually Conner rode in his chair in the back, but this was a special occasion.

The puppy galloped into Conner's seat before he could even buckle up. "Oh, wow! He's enormous!" Conner scooped up their monster of a pup, holding her away from his face as she slurped the air and wiggled wildly.

"She. *She* was the largest puppy in the whole litter." Marcus crossed his fingers. Would Conner like the puppy he'd picked? The pup escaped and attacked Conner's face with licks. Then she moved to his ears, cleaning each one as though it were in dire need of some serious scrubbing.

"She's awesome, and huge. I didn't think the puppies would be this big."

"Hmmm, yeah, me neither. But I checked with Mom and she'd already paid and everything. She definitely said to bring one home."

"Let's name her Moose. Here Moose, Moose, Moose."

The puppy finished Conner's ears and moved on to washing his eyebrows. The boys tried everything from "Dire Bear" to "Sam," but the puppy continued bathing Conner. Marcus wasn't surprised. Conner was seriously filthy. Dust and paint splattered his clothes and hair.

"What did they call her at the breeder's?"

"Oh, mostly Phooey Kerflooey for short," Marcus answered.

Their puppy's head came up and her heavy ears pricked slightly. She wagged her tail and scratched at Marcus's knee with one paw as though congratulating him for getting her name right.

"Oh, that's not going to work. What about MonsterJaws?" Conner smiled and patted the monster jawbreaker he kept in his sweatshirt pouch.

The pup started cleaning Conner's elbow then slurped down his arm until her snout was buried inside the front pouch of his sweatshirt. She rooted around, then popped up, wagging furiously with the huge jawbreaker clutched in her mouth.

"Gross!" Conner snatched the giant candy away, wiping it on his shirt. "What was Phooey Kerflooey short for? It's not a very short name."

The puppy paused, ears pricked once more. She gave a happy yip and wagged.

"Are you sure you want to know?"

Conner scowled. "Of course. It couldn't be that bad."

"We could shorten it to Phooey."

"No, just tell me what they named her."

"Princess Foo Foo Bear," Marcus whispered. The whispering didn't help.

At the sound of her old name, Phooey leapt off of Conner's lap and her front paws hit Marcus smack in the chest. She wiggled and wagged, slurped and bounced, turned in wild circles and then flopped down on her back for a belly rub.

Conner choked. It took a few tries before he got himself breathing properly again. "Oh, wow. Phooey it is! Anything but . . . you know, 'the name that must not be spoken.'"

Aunt Stella pulled up to a small brick jewelry store just a few blocks from home. "Now you boys keep the furbaby happy while I grab your momma's surprise and something special for dinner."

She trundled across the street to place their order at The Sassy Sasquatch Café. Then hurried to the nearest shop and heaved open the antique glass door. The shop's name, "The Gilded Blossom," was written in fancy gold lettering on the door, along with a single glittering rose. A small brass bell dinged as she entered.

It didn't take long before Aunt Stella was back. She carried three large paper sacks that smelled of garlic, hot oil, and baked apples in one hand and a fancy black gift bag with gold lettering in the other.

Aunt Stella heaved herself into the seat and then lay back panting. "Goodness, these vans are tall. Now look here, boys." She snapped open a small velvet box.

Marcus and Conner had scoured magazines with Dad before settling on a birthday gift for Mom: a mother's ring. There, on a bed of black silk lay the most beautiful ring Marcus had ever seen. It had Mom's birthstone in the middle, a fancy lacework of gold, and an opal birthstone for Marcus on one side and a turquoise for Conner on the other. He couldn't wait to see Mom's eyes brighten at the fancy gift.

Someone else's eyes brightened at the appearance of the ring.

Phooey leaned across Conner's lap for a closer look. She cocked her head to the side and gave a low huff deep in her throat.

"Do you want to see, girl?" Conner held her closer and Phooey gave him a grateful wag.

She leaned farther out and pressed her nose close to the velvet box.

Marcus grinned. Phooey already had something in common with Mom: a love of pretty things. His plan was going perfectly. Big and fluffy for Conner, and a girl who liked fancy stuff, just like Mom.

Phooey gave a gentle sniff and paused over the gleaming piece of jewelry. After a silent moment of appreciation, she lunged forward and slurped the ring into her mouth.

Aunt Stella screamed.

Conner gagged in horror.

Marcus was left to act.

He plunged his whole hand into Phooey's gooey maw, questing around for the tiny ring. There, in the slobber pocket at the side of her jowl. Phooey struggled and growled, clearly determined to snork down the expensive gift. Marcus pinned her flat with one arm and hooked the ring with a finger.

Phooey clamped down on his hand. A fierce wrestling match followed that ended with Marcus holding the dripping ring high in triumph.

Phooey howled and retreated to Conner's lap. She turned her back on Marcus, sat with a humph, and buried her face in his brother's chest.

Marcus wiped off the ring on his shirt, leaving a wet smear, then tucked Mom's gift back into the slot in the silk fabric.

After a silent journey through town, wherein Phooey refused to look at him, they finally pulled into the drive and Aunt Stella turned off the van.

"Let's get you into the house, Conner, and then we can all admire this little fuzzball." She held the ring box tight, even as she gave Phooey a gentle pat. Aunt Stella brought around Conner's empty chair and then paused to peer at a yellow sign next door in front of Nia's yard. The grass was crowded with tables and lamps and a fancy old couch.

"Marcus, would you hand me my purse?" Aunt Stella helped Conner out of the van. "There's a big yard sale at that cute little neighbor girl's house. I'll just be a minute."

Aunt Stella snatched her purse and hustled down their long driveway toward Nia's.

Marcus didn't think she'd have called Nia a "cute little girl" if she'd ever faced her on the paintball field.

Behind him, Phooey wedged her snout through the van door and wriggled her rump, preparing for a leap to freedom.

"Oh, no you don't. Not till I get your leash on." He plopped her into the driver's seat and paused. It wasn't hot today, she would be fine, He scattered a handful of kibble around her big paws. "You work on that while I help Conner."

Marcus looked around. Never mind. Conner was already on the move.

His brother gave a whoop and wheeled toward the house. "Let me get all the dog toys. Phooey's gonna love the squeaky spider."

Just then, Aunt Stella waved her arms wildly from Nia's driveway. Marcus slid the van door shut so

Phooey wouldn't escape and jogged down the narrow asphalt strip until he made it to Nia's.

"Just look at these! Haven't seen one in years. I'm getting one for each of the bathrooms. What colors do you think your mother would like?"

Marcus stared at a small card table where Nia's mom had set up an alarming display of crocheted bathroom accessories in a variety of pastel shades. But these were even worse than furry toilet seat covers or doilies meant to sit beneath a toothbrush holder. Wide-eyed dolls with spidery eyelashes, fluffy hair, and stiff plastic faces gazed back at him. Each doll wore an enormous crocheted ball gown. Now Marcus understood Nia's panicked tone when she'd said her mom was "obsessed with antique crochet patterns."

"Look!" Aunt Stella lifted the corner of a lacy pink dress. Instead of stiff doll legs, there was a roll of toilet paper under the skirt. "It's for the spare TP, on the back of the toilet."

Ah . . . Apparently, you were supposed to put the dolls legs into a TP roll and the floofy dress would spread over the toilet paper, making it look all fancy.

Marcus grimaced. There was no particular color that would make the TP dolls look less horrifying.

"Mom's bathroom has green in it," Marcus mumbled. Hopefully, she wouldn't remember that the boys also had a bathroom. Why couldn't Aunt Stella buy the towering stack of jazz records, some fancy dishtowels, that figurine of an African American angel with a shiny pearl halo, or even one of Nia's homemade guinea pig toys?

Aunt Stella snatched up four. "Two for me and two for your mom. Now, that pup isn't in the van with our food, right?"

The food!

Marcus gulped and spun around. He sprinted up their driveway, back toward the van. How could he have forgotten Phooey and the food?

Marcus hauled open the door and froze. There were wads of waxed paper, empty ketchup packets, and torn takeout boxes everywhere. The hot, oily scent of fries and ground beef permeated the air.

Where was Phooey?

A bag under the seat rustled.

Marcus crouched.

The largest paper sack was moving around the floor. A black tail poked out the end. It was wagging steadily.

Marcus yanked the sack off their pup.

Phooey met his gaze. She had a plastic cup of coleslaw in the side of her mouth and her eyes actually appeared to be sparkling with delight.

"No, drop it!"

Phooey's eyes lost their sparkle and took on a flinty gleam. She growled and clamped down on the coleslaw.

Marcus dove.

Phooey darted under the seat.

Marcus army-crawled after their pup as fast as he could.

Finally, Aunt Stella huffed up the driveway. "What happened?" She leaned against the van, gasping for breath.

"Phooey ate the food, but I saved this coleslaw." Marcus poked his head out from under the seat and held up the badly dented tub of mayonnaise-drenched cabbage.

Aunt Stella's eyes paused on the tooth marks that marred the clear plastic.

"She ate three deluxe hamburgers?"

"Yes."

"Three large orders of garlic fries?"

"Yes."

"Three large slices of apple pie, with ice cream and caramel sauce?"

"Yes, plus a dozen ketchup packets." He wasn't upset about the ketchup, but Marcus's stomach groaned when she mentioned the pie.

"And then she had the gall to eat three servings of coleslaw."

"No. She only ate two. I saved this one." Marcus offered her the crunched plastic tub again. Aunt Stella shook her head and turned away, marching into the house without a reply.

Marcus scowled down at Phooey. She had fallen asleep flopped on the seat with her belly to the sky. Her very round belly.

A puppy was supposed to fix things. Bring a breath of peace into their chaos. What happened to puppy-snuggling and calm? What happened to Conner drawing comics instead of jumping his chair over the frog statues at the park? What happened to Dad sleeping all night instead of watching for Conner to escape again and Mom not having to investigate every time she heard a muffled thump on the roof?

What happened to their perfect peace?

"You did not make friends with that stunt, Phooey."

The pup sneezed once and then began to snore.

Phooey Kerflooey, indeed. Marcus had asked the flannel lady to look up the strange word "Kerflooey" on her phone. It was an adverb that meant to cease functioning, especially suddenly and completely, to fall apart, or to fail. What part of their puppy adventure would go kerflooey next?

Marcus stuffed her ballerina doll under his shirt to hide it from Conner. They had some fierce and brave toys that she would like better, like the squeaky alien. He heaved their huge pup into his arms and struggled to carry Phooey into the house without dropping her.

Marcus set Phooey down on the floor mat by the kitchen door. Conner barreled toward them down the hall. The thrum of the playing cards and flashing patterns of the Monkey Light Conner had clipped in the spokes of his wheelchair filled the hallway as he zoomed up behind them. The lights were really bright at night, but even in the daylight the flashing colors were overwhelming.

Marcus had found a way to fix Conner's chair up with a cup holder, umbrella, book bag, and portable lantern, and was still working on a leash attachment so he could walk Phooey.

Phooey jerked awake as the flashing, thrumming, umbrella-toting wheelchair approached her. She froze with her paws splayed out. Her eyes widened and her tail drooped. She let out a mournful howl. Phooey tried to scramble away so fast she ran in place for just a moment making the mat heap up under her paws before she thundered off.

"Gracious gophers!" Aunt Stella stared after Phooey, her hand covering her mouth. "Don't worry, she can't go far."

They all heard a thump from the back door.

"The dog door!" Conner shouted.

All three of them rushed through the house.

Phooey Kerflooey

Sure enough, there in the middle of the back door was Phooey. At least the back end of Phooey. The door was for a smaller dog and she was wedged partway through.

"Poor girl! Here, let me help." Conner wheeled closer, but the cards thrummed, the Monkey Light flashed, and the folded umbrella he'd reattached after paintball made a swooshing noise.

Phooey pushed madly with her back paws and then shot out the door.

Marcus bent and peered through. There she was, panting and running and—oh, wow, was she chasing that awful squirrel?

No, wait. Rasputin was chasing Phooey.

"Watch out, she's coming back!" Marcus scrambled away from the dog door just in time.

Phooey rocketed through, the squirrel right behind her. The furry rodent was actually baring his blunt little teeth at their huge and "ferocious" dog.

The squirrel scampered closer and nipped the tip of Phooey's tail.

"Unhand our dog," Conner shouted. "You starveling, you stock-fish, you dried neat's tongue!"

Their pup yowled and launched away. She scrambled up into Conner's lap, realized that she was in the terrifying chair, and just kept on climbing.

Phooey was up Conner's chest in a flash, but caught sight of the umbrella and whimpered. She hurtled off Conner's shoulder and sailed through the air, paws churning as though she might run across the clouds like some cartoon character who had yet to look down.

It didn't work. She reached the highest point of her leap and then plummeted. With a crash, she hit the garbage can and disappeared inside.

It was silent for a moment and then the garbage exploded.

Food scraps and coffee grounds flew skyward as Phooey burst out of the trash. Grit and banana peels rained down upon them. Phooey hit the linoleum and spun in a circle on the slippery floor, her legs splatted out like a giant furry starfish.

She stared at the slick flooring, scrambled to her feet and slipped, slewed, fell. Then propelled herself around the corner, howling.

CHAPTER EIGHT
Phooey is Afraid

Marcus found Phooey under his parents' bed.

She lay flat against the floor with her big head resting on her paws. Her whole body was trembling. "Come on, girl." Marcus reached but could barely feel a brush of fluff at his fingertips. He needed another strategy.

His brother was in the hall when Marcus jogged past on his way to the kitchen. Conner grumbled as he tore the cards and lights and little glowing stars off his wheelchair. Aunt Stella was heating up alphabet soup for dinner and muttering about their missing pie under her breath.

Marcus opened the fridge and looked around for something special. They hadn't bought any puppy treats yet. There, in the back of a drawer, the end of a cheese block had a tiny bit of mold on it. Mom always cut that off and threw it away. The cheese would be perfect.

Phooey did not like moldy cheese. She didn't like lunch meat, either, or hot dogs. Marcus pulled out every single package from the fridge. One of them promised all-natural sliced turkey without preservatives of any kind. He snatched up a slice and took it to Phooey's hiding place.

Phooey gave a delicate sniff, licked her chops, and then oozed out from under the bed toward the all-natural lunchmeat like some kind of furry worm.

Marcus dragged the slice across the floor, making a tantalizing scent trail. He was a little worried that he'd have to scrub meat juice off the carpet until he saw that Phooey was happy to take care of the mess.

She slurped her way toward him, her tongue working overtime.

He gathered Phooey into his arms and gave her a moment to gobble down her treat. Then Marcus lugged her outside for multiple potty breaks. All of which required lots of pats, encouragement, and Marcus standing right beside her as she gave everything in the yard a suspicious side-eye.

The boys gulped down a bowl of soup and saltine crackers. Aunt Stella gave Phooey a few pats, but continued to mumble things that sounded like, "Deluxe burger . . . all those crispy fries . . . enough pie to choke a mule."

Phooey did not appear weighted down by the guilt of her crimes. Instead of hanging her head whenever Aunt Stella mumbled about the pilfered burgers, she eyed their soup and poked her nose suggestively toward a cracker that rested near the edge of the table.

However, she had no interest whatsoever in the shiny food and water dishes Marcus set on the floor next to the kitchen island. Her tongue lolled out the side of her mouth like she must be thirsty, but still she turned her nose up at the bowl of water. Instead, she followed the boys around the kitchen, staring at their mugs and whining every time they took a sip.

Conner put his mug on the floor and she galloped forward, wagging. Then she skidded to a stop and flinched back. Phooey's ears flattened. She hid behind a kitchen chair.

"I think she just insulted my bear mug," Conner said.

"She can't understand the pictures. Let's try another."

Phooey turned up her nose at Mom's heart mug, Dad's spaceship mug, Aunt Stella's Knitting Olympics mug, and Marcus's 1st place "Math Monster" mug. When Phooey's panting got so loud that Aunt Stella started looking up "alarming medical symptoms" on a veterinary website, Marcus hand-fed her ice cubes until her tail got some of its wag back.

She didn't eat any dog food, either. That wasn't surprising after her stolen feast, but she did gallop off with Aunt Stella's soup spoon.

At least they'd fed and watered their new dog, if ice cubes, a heap of hamburgers, and a spoon counted as responsible pet care. Perhaps Phooey was just riled up from her first day. Once she was well-rested,

Phooey would look more like the perfect puppy Mom and Conner had expected.

While Phooey was busy growling at Conner's bear mug again, Marcus zoomed his brother down the hall so they could brush their teeth. He smeared toothpaste at a reckless speed and glanced into the hall as they brushed and spit and brushed again. "Hurry!" He nudged Conner when his brother stopped to put goop in his hair to make it stick out in all directions. "Aunt Stella won't be in the kitchen long and I don't want Phooey to be alone."

Conner scowled, and put the hair goop back. "What could happen? You shut the sliding door so she's trapped in the kitchen."

A terrible crash echoed through the house.

Marcus bolted down the hall. Conner propelled his chair at breakneck speed right behind.

Phooey wasn't sprawled at the edge of the linoleum growling at the bear mug. She wasn't on the table licking the butter dish clean, although its shiny emptiness indicated that she'd done so recently. Nope, she was sitting in the kitchen sink surrounded by broken dishes with her head stuck in the mug rack, howling and howling and howling.

"I thought you didn't like any of those mugs?" Marcus cuddled Phooey close and lugged her into their bedroom, while Conner wheeled after them. Marcus cuddled her in the hallway while Conner got out of his chair using the handy straps Dad had hung from the ceiling.

Even so, Phooey cringed back when she spotted the wheelchair in the corner. Even without all of Conner's doodads, she trembled at the sight of it.

Conner tossed a blanked over his chair and settled back into a pile of pillows on the bottom bunk

Marcus sat down on the bed beside his brother and slowly released his grip on Phooey.

She galumphed over to Conner and plopped onto his chest, wagging her tail and slurping his nose.

So it wasn't Conner she was afraid of, just his chair—and the squirrel, and the mugs, and apparently lunch meat with chemicals.

Phooey stretched out on the bed, wiggling around until she took up most of the space.

Conner stroked her soft fur and silky ears, slowly sinking toward sleep.

Marcus smiled. They could start training their pup in the morning. Right now, all he wanted to do was enjoy this peaceful moment together. They finally had a dog of their own and she was already calming his brother. What a good girl.

Phooey flopped onto her back with her paws in the air. When nothing happened, she rolled her head to the side so that she was looking right at Marcus. She sniffed and sort of raised one eyebrow.

Oh yeah, belly rubs. He scratched her tummy.

Slowly, slowly Phooey relaxed until she was just a limp mound of fur, snoring and twitching her back paw.

Marcus's head drooped onto one of Conner's pillows. He scratched slower and slower until only one tired finger was barely scritching Phooey's belly.

OK, bedtime. Marcus stopped scratching.

Phooey twitched. Her eyes popped open. Her ears tilted to an indignant angle and she began to cry. Not a howl, but not quite a bark, either. The sound was terrible. A sad, warbling song of discontent and longing. The meaning was clear. More belly rubs!

Marcus rushed to scratch her tummy.

Phooey sagged with fatigue and her breathing slowed. Almost . . . almost asleep. Maybe one more minute and she would be out.

Conner moved slightly in bed.

Phooey thrashed around to get comfy against Marcus's brother. She wriggled and kicked her paws in the air. Phooey wormed hither and yon until she rested with her head pillowed on Conner's right leg, her tail draped over his left, and all four paws skyward so that her belly was conveniently situated for more scratching. She lay motionless for a moment.

Marcus breathed out a relieved sigh. Surely he could move her to the crate now.

Phooey's brown eyes popped open and met his gaze. She waited, raising one eyebrow and twitching an ear. One twitch, two . . . She appeared to be waiting.

Marcus scratched her tummy.

Phooey relaxed, sinking into the bed like an old toy whose stuffing had settled.

OK, maybe two more minutes . . .

As soon as Marcus paused to rest his aching hand, Phooey's plaintive howls resumed. Louder and louder she cried, loud enough that Conner woke up and Aunt Stella shuffled down the hall to check on them.

Conner groaned and pulled himself up using the loops Dad had bolted to the underside of the bunk. He rubbed his eyes and blinked down at the crying puppy. "Let's read her a story."

Marcus considered the row of worn picture books on Conner's shelf. They'd been shoved to the back as adventure novels replaced their childhood read-alouds. It probably didn't matter what they read to her. Just the sound of his voice should be soothing.

Conner blearily pointed in the general direction of an old favorite, the story of David and Goliath.

Marcus scooted over so Phooey rested between them. He smoothed a hand over the book's sun-bleached dust jacket before turning to the first page.

"Once upon a time, there was a young shepherd boy who loved every single sheep in his care."

Phooey cocked an ear, let out a sigh, and wiggled deeper into the covers.

"He led them to quiet pools to drink and battled lions and bears to protect them. He was a good shepherd, but his father and brothers needed him just as much as his sheep. For far away, in a deep valley, an army gathered."

Phooey's tail twitched and she flopped over so that one eye stared wide at Marcus.

Weird. It almost looked as though she understood that the story was taking a frightening turn. There was no way she could have, though. It had to be the tension that had crept into his voice. Marcus tried to make the words soothing and low, even as the tale grew perilous.

"A giant warrior strode to the front of the enemy troops."

Phooey struggled until she lay upright with both ears pricked.

"The giant stood at a great height, nine-and-a-half feet tall. He was clad in scale armor so heavy it would have made a normal man sink to his knees. His spear was too massive for any but himself to wield."

The fur between Phooey's shoulder blades bristled and a low growl rumbled in her chest.

Marcus glanced up from the story. There was no way she could understand, and yet . . . Her eyes were so wide that the whites showed, and her lip was pulled back in a snarl.

He shook his head and returned to the story. "The giant drove his spear into the ground and stood with legs splayed wide. 'I defy the ranks of Israel today. Choose a man and let him come down to me. If he is able to kill me, then we become your servants; but if I prevail, you shall become our servants.' Now the people trembled at the warrior Goliath's great size and might, but the shepherd boy David gripped his sling and asked: 'Who is this Philistine, that he should taunt the armies of the living God?'"

Phooey shuddered and Marcus pulled her close as he read the part where David was taken before King Saul, who offered the hand of his daughter in marriage and an amazing tax rebate to anyone who would slay the giant and free Israel from Philistine oppression.

As king Saul attempted to force David to use his ill-fitting armor for the battle, Marcus glanced back over the story. David had a pretty chaotic life, too. A dad who'd forgotten about him when Samuel came to visit, a bunch of upset brothers, and now a giant? How had David ignored the chaos around him and faced the giant alone?

"David walked down to where the giant stood, gripping a simple sling and five smooth stones. The giant looked down upon David and laughed, for he realized that the great warrior of Israel was only a boy. 'Am I a dog that you come to me with sticks?' Goliath cursed David and strode forward with weapons in hand, prepared to slay the insolent boy who dared to trust that God, Himself, would win the fight."

Phooey let out a mournful howl, her snout raised high in the air and her furry lip quivering. Conner blinked sleepy eyes and sat up. "What's wrong, girl?"

Phooey whimpered then dove off the bed. She hit the floor with a thump, scrambled upright, and galloped away, howling all the while.

Wow, maybe she did understand the story.

Marcus searched three rooms before he found their pup quivering beneath a couch cushion. He scooped up Phooey and toted her to the dog crate they'd set up in the laundry room. It was full of cuddly stuffed animals, a hot water bottle, and a ticking alarm clock. Phooey did not approve. She cried until Marcus plopped down beside the crate, opened the wire door, and began to rub her belly once more.

After Phooey woke from a sound sleep four more times, Marcus gave up. He yanked a pillow and puffy quilt off his bunk and stumbled back to the laundry room. He mounded the bedding into a nest just outside the crate and snuggled up with one arm stretched out far enough to reach their insomniac pup.

Alrighty then, more belly rubs. Maybe once she was in a really deep sleep, he could sneak off to his bunk.

CHAPTER NINE
Phooey Needs a Cheering Squad to go Potty

The kitchen clock chimed midnight, yanking Marcus out of a painful slumber. Why did his neck hurt, and his arm, and the fingers of his right hand? He dragged his eyelids open and glanced around. The laundry room? He squinted through the dark at his aching arm and realized why everything hurt. He was still scratching Phooey's belly, even in his sleep.

Marcus stopped scratching.

Phooey bolted upright, wide awake.

"It's time to take you potty, girl," he mumbled, rubbing the knots out of his aching arm.

Phooey plopped her head on the edge of the crate, her loose jowls sagged around her face and her big eyes stared up with rapt attention.

She was really cute. Maybe even cute enough that sleeping on the floor to rub her belly made sense.

Marcus consulted the dog-training book. He was supposed to carry her outside so that an accident didn't happen the minute she left the crate. He scooped up the twenty-two-pound pup and staggered toward the back door. Maybe she should use the doggy door while she still could. It would be too small soon. Marcus set Phooey down in front of the dog door.

Phooey lowered her head and peered at the small, black rectangle. She gave a concerned whine and bolted.

"Don't pee, please don't pee." Marcus charged after her. "Come on, Phooey, you can make it outside." He caught her near the newly upholstered couch in the living room and scooped her up fast.

Mom's latest design had required a pale purple linen for the couch and both overstuffed chairs. It looked nice with the light gray carpeting, soft decorative blankets, and lacy wall hangings, but he was pretty sure that slobber, dog hair, and a huge puddle of pee would be noticeable against the new fabric. If Phooey wrecked Mom's showcase room, Mom would be much more likely to remember that she'd expected a four-pound puppy, not a twenty-two-pound Sasquatch.

A captive once more, Phooey made a sad noise. It was half sigh and half whine.

"It's OK, girl. I'll carry you through the big door. Just don't have an accident."

Marcus lugged their monster pup down the hall and through the back door. He set her down on the patio. "Go on. The rocks are over there." Phooey didn't budge. She braced her paws, lowered her head, and peered into the darkness. A cricket chirped. Oh, cool! He would have to tell Conner that they did have bugs. Phooey was not excited about the newly discovered crickets.

The pup simply disappeared.

Marcus turned in a circle looking for her. How could such a large animal move so quietly? The swinging dog door gave him a pretty good idea which direction their brave guard dog had headed.

The next time, Marcus set her down right on the decorative rocks and then jumped back on the patio where his bare feet wouldn't be so cold.

Phooey jumped onto the patio, too, sitting down with a plop right beside him. She looked out at the dark night and then up at Marcus. What did she think he could do about it? The crickets weren't going to stop singing just because she was scared. Although, if she just needed company . . .

Marcus scooped Phooey up again, plopped her onto the rocks, and stayed beside her.

Phooey gave a happy sigh and started sniffing around.

Marcus hopped from one foot to the other, hoping she would hurry it up. "Go potty, Phooey," he said. "Go potty." The dog-training book said that if the dog could associate a word with going outside, training would go faster since she would know why they had come out. The book also mentioned how puppies needed lots of encouragement.

Marcus looked around. No one was watching. He started out with a few basic encouragements. "You are such a good girl, Phooey. I bet you can pee more than all the puppies in your litter. Speaking of litter, you don't even need a box like a cat. Dogs are so brave, going potty outside. Good girl!"

Phooey sat and looked up at him, wagging just the tip of her tail. Was that her way of telling him to keep the praise coming?

Maybe a little song, just this once.

Hmmm . . . Mom used to sing "Hush Little Baby" when they were small. Marcus leaned down close and made his voice soothing and happy. "Hush little puppy, you can pee, maybe over there beside that tree." It was actually a fencepost, but she didn't know that.

Phooey's wagging sped up.

Marcus pointed toward the post. "Hush little puppy, it's not hard, you can go potty in the yard."

Phooey paused next to the fencepost and looked up at him expectantly.

One more verse maybe. "Hush little puppy, you must make a puddle, or without sleep my head will be a muddle."

Finally, Phooey squatted in the rocks.

"Go potty, go potty!" Marcus gave her a piece of cheese, non-moldy this time.

Phooey sniffed the morsel, gave the treat a cautious lick, and gulped the cheese down. Then she took off for the edge of the yard, turned at the corner and hurtled back. Around and around and around she went, faster and faster with Marcus chasing behind. All of a sudden she sat, skidded across the rocks, and slumped over onto her side. She rolled once and then curled into a ball.

Oh no! Marcus fell to his knees beside their puppy. He felt her soft sides and examined her for wounds.

Her body rose and fell with deep breaths. She was curled up tight in a furry ball. A snorting snore escaped, then another.

Wow, chapter five in the dog book was right. Puppies really did fall asleep fast.

Marcus carried her back to her crate and settled their big pup onto an old towel inside.

Now for his secret mission. He crept to the corner of the laundry room where he'd stashed Phooey's backpack.

There was no way to make a ballerina doll look fierce. He tugged out Phooey's doll, tiptoed outside, and stuffed it deep into the outdoor garbage underneath the remains of their box fort. The garbage was overflowing so he had to mash it down and then stomp on the top to make it fit. He heard a crack, but that was all right. It wasn't like either he or Conner would ever come looking for Phooey's ridiculous non-ferocious toy. He tiptoed back, ready to fall into bed. Phooey rolled on her back, belly up, and began to cry.

Oh yeah, belly rubs.

Marcus sighed, flopped on the floor beside her, and began to scratch her tummy.

CHAPTER TEN
The Squirrel Attacks and Phooey Does Not

Aunt Stella's wild shouts of "Gracious gophers!" woke Marcus the next morning. His whole arm was numb from scratching Phooey. It hung lifeless at his side as he stumbled from the laundry room.

Rasputin the squirrel had apparently found the doggy door and used the handy entrance to stage a full home invasion. While Aunt Stella shouted and ran about waving a broom, Rasputin terrorized the kitchen as though the creature was working down a checklist of havoc.

Flour: tipped over and scattered across the counters—check.

Cornmeal: dumped onto the stove top—check.

Bread and tortillas: nibbled and chewed—check.

Garbage: tipped and scattered—check.

Counters: pooed on and ransacked—check.

Decorative vase: broken, and flowers dragged across the floor—check.

Aunt Stella: near insane with fury—check.

Conner: using every Shakespearian insult he knew, even "You fustilarian!"—check.

Marcus cringed. Would Mom think that Phooey was to blame? No, Aunt Stella herself was witness to Rasputin's attack. The terrible mess had nothing whatsoever to do with their new dog. Mom would be upset, but at least the squirrel was in the kitchen, not the redesigned living room.

He glanced around. How much would a woodland animal charge for this much rampant destruction? Rasputin had apparently done it all for the pure fun of it. A pro bono rampage. How generous.

Aunt Stella swung her broom wildly. The fluffy-tailed villain leapt from counter to stove to fridge in a flash. Aunt Stella looked like a Viking warrior in a berserker rage.

Marcus debated the safest way to offer aid without accidentally being whomped by the broom, when Conner barreled past him and into the war zone.

"Here, Aunt Stella, let me help!"

She spun around, broom aloft, eyes blazing, then got ahold of herself. "We've got to catch this squirrel before eight o'clock or we'll be late for church." She paused to lean against the doorway, gasping for breath.

Marcus glanced at the clock. They had fifteen minutes.

These were indeed desperate times. OK then, desperate measures were called for. How to catch a marauding squirrel?

"Take the corner by the fridge, Conner," Aunt Stella said. "Marcus, you guard the door. If only we had one more person to stand in the pantry corner, we'd have him for sure."

A sleepy Phooey wandered into the kitchen, nose sniffing, tail wagging.

Oh no, she must have smelled the eggs that were smashed on the floor.

Phooey Kerflooey

Phooey trundled to the edge of the kitchen mat, nose in the air, heading straight for the shattered eggs. Upon seeing the carton, she gave a delighted yip and plunged into the gooey mess, snout first.

The only problem, another furry predator had already claimed the eggs and was currently feeding at his kill.

Rasputin's head popped up from behind the carton. His tail twitched in a menacing fashion and his beady little eyes grew intent and dangerous. Then, with a shrill cry, the squirrel attacked.

Phooey scrambled backwards with a yelp.

The squirrel sensed weakness and made good his threat. He flicked his fluffy tail and darted forward, biting the twenty-two-pound puppy right on the nose.

Phooey cried out in pain, tucked her tail between her legs, and scrambled for the door.

But the squirrel wasn't finished. That furry woodland creature sprang onto their doggy's head and clawed and bit and scampered and scolded until Phooey was a gibbering mass of pure panic.

When the critter dug its little claws into her backside and actually chomped down on Phooey's floppy tail, she lost it. Literally. Phooey fled the kitchen howling and yipping, leaving a puddle in her wake.

Today, Marcus had planned to take Phooey to the park for the first time and socialize her with ducks, kids, and other dogs.

Aunt Stella had promised to make cinnamon rolls to celebrate Phooey's arrival.

Their parents were expecting to video chat that evening to hear about the new puppy.

None of these calm and delightful activities occurred. They didn't even make it to church, although Aunt Stella did shout the Lord's name loudly on several occasions while flinging her arms skyward. She must have been praying . . . a lot.

Instead of the park, cinnamon rolls, and pleasant chats, they chased Rasputin all day long.

When the squirrel wasn't in the kitchen darting through spilled cornmeal, he was in the bathroom chewing up rolls of toilet paper. When he wasn't in the bathroom, he was in the attic shattering Christmas tree ornaments. After he'd completed a thorough ransacking of the attic, the squirrel progressed to the guestroom and indulged in chewing into Aunt Stella's recliner, then pulling stuffing out in great messy hunks. He then scampered into Marcus and Conner's room to chew on handcrafted game cards and poo right in the middle of their pillows as though daring them to do something about his pillaging ways.

They caught Rasputin there—for all of five minutes.

Conner yanked the door shut while Phooey cowered under the bed.

Marcus attempted to herd Rasputin into a garbage can with a battered hockey stick.

However, closed doors and old sporting equipment were no match for a squirrel with havoc on his mind. While they searched for better squirrel wrangling tools, Rasputin nibbled a tiny hole next to the window molding. When they finally found him again, Rasputin simply darted into his getaway hole and disappeared into the wall.

They were completely helpless in the face of the tiny creature's wild destruction.

Rasputin was lightning fast, darting first one way and then the next. He could climb bookshelves and leap off the TV. He could run along curtain rods and scamper across the tops of doors. The horrible animal could even claw his way up Marcus's pant leg and leap from the top of his head to Conner's and then down onto Phooey's back, causing another yowl of terror and big puddle on the floor.

That was the other problem. Not only could no one catch the squirrel, no one could catch Phooey, either. Their pup was insane with terror and determined to do everything necessary to keep a safe distance from the ferocious rodent.

Which led to the next problem.

Aunt Stella was focused on trying to clean up all the spilled stuff that lay scattered in the squirrel's wake. So, she had charged the boys with animal control. Find and catch Phooey. Find and catch the squirrel. There were two boys and two rampaging beasts. It should have been simple.

It wasn't.

The squirrel seemed to know Phooey was afraid. He even appeared to take delight in tormenting her.

The only good thing was that the squirrel had not found his way into Mom's sacred domain: the showcase living room.

As Conner herded Rasputin to the bathroom, where the squirrel darted into the medicine cabinet and inexplicably disappeared, the doorbell rang.

Marcus waited for Aunt Stella to hear and answer. The only sound she uttered was a muffled shout followed by the thump of a broom against linoleum. Hmmm . . . not encouraging. Marcus gulped and opened the sliding pocket door that separated the living room from the rest of the house so he could answer the door. Phooey squeezed through right as he was sliding it shut.

He scooped up their big pup, approached the front door, and cautiously turned the knob.

He opened it to Nia's mom, a tall lady with a fancy braided bun. She gasped and placed one hand over her heart. Nia bounced on the stoop, peering around her mom.

Oh, no! What had Nia's mom seen? Had Rasputin just gotten into the living room and pulled the stuffing from Mom's perfect couch?

"Your mother is a genius, young man." Nia's mom took a sip from a china teacup she'd brought with her as she peeked into the room from the doorway. "That pale lavender is heavenly with all those smokey gray accents."

Marcus sagged with relief, then pushed his glasses up higher on his nose. Smokey gray accents he could handle. "Come on in, Mrs. Williams."

Nia followed her mom with a clatter as her braids swung against her shoulders. She bent over Phooey and let the pup slobber her face while she fired off a string of chatter. "I had no idea Scottish terriers were so ginormous! What are you feeding him? Did Conner absolutely and totally love the Rube Goldberg machine?"

Marcus gave them the tour, his heart pounding harder with each step. This was a common scenario. No matter which wheelchair-safe house they lived in, the neighborhood ladies soon knew that the living room was for business. Mom encouraged them to stop by any time, especially during the first week of the month when she had a new design on display.

A thump rattled the door that divided them from the hall and the sound of a wheelchair barreling away was followed by an almost indecipherable chitter.

"Yes," Marcus said in a loud and super cheerful voice. So cheerful that Nia gave him a suspicious look. "I especially like the moths and pressed flowers." Mom had searched far and wide for artwork in various shades of gray and finally hit the jackpot with an amateur oil painter from a local coffee shop who had a fascination for moths resting on dried flowers.

"So, where's your brother?" Nia glanced around as though Conner might burst out from under the sofa at any moment.

Marcus raised his eyebrows at Nia, hoping she would understand and stop asking questions. "He's resting." He faked a smile and motioned vaguely toward the back of the house. Did being trapped in a corner by a barricade of pillows and fighting off a squirrel with a plunger count as resting? Pillows were involved so . . . maybe? Marcus tried not to think too hard about the truthfulness of that statement.

Nia bent closer and rubbed her nose against Phooey's soft fur. "So, what'd you name the puppy?"

"Um," Marcus squeezed Phooey tighter as a trilling cry sounded from the other side of the sliding door. "Her name is Phooey."

"Oh, my goodness! You got a girl puppy!"

Nia was a lot more excited than Marcus had expected. Maybe she needed her own dog instead of two squeaky guinea pigs and that grumpy cat who didn't like ribbons.

"Every kid on this street is a boy," Nia said. "There isn't a girl my age in the whole neighborhood."

Huh? He hadn't noticed. Then again, when Conner tried to sneak out in his wheelchair to play street hockey after bedtime, he'd never lacked an accomplice. Now that Marcus thought about it, there were a lot of other boys.

"She's not your age, Nia. Plus, she's a dog. I'm pretty sure she's not going to enjoy playing salon any more than that monster cat of yours."

Phooey slobbered Nia's ear and wagged.

"Nefurious is just old. He would enjoy brushing more if he didn't have arthritis . . . and if I hadn't gotten nail polish all over his ear that time. I was such a kid back then. I'll be super gentle. I have a whole new collection of hair bows and even some glitter." Nia smiled in a way that had Marcus looking for an escape route.

Phooey's wagging increased to warp speed. Surely she didn't want glitter? What sane animal would? Encouraging Nia's horrendous plans for their dog would probably traumatize Phooey and infuriate Conner. Maybe he could lock the door and shut off all the lights when Nia came over next?

"Grandma is up from Georgia and Mom will bring her over later," Nia said. "They want to spruce up our house before we sell. You know, if Dad gets that job."

"Wait, your dad is interviewing for a new job? That's so weird. Our dad is, too."

"Yeah, I know. They drove up together. Anyway . . . " Nia ruffled Phooey's ears as though she hadn't just dropped vital intel about their parents into the conversation. "I'll bring my whole pet salon and we can find out what kind of grooming routine your puppy prefers. It'll be great. Like having a little sister!" Nia kissed Phooey on the nose.

No, no, no! Phooey wasn't a little sister. She was a large and ferocious—well, soon-to-be ferocious—dog. But now was not the time to correct Nia's presumptions about Phooey. If only he could find out more about this mystery job of Dad's . . .

More skittering and a shout from Conner launched Marcus into action.

Nia's mom was easily distracted by the moth paintings and how the velvety blankets looked kind of like melting chocolate the way they had been arranged in pooling folds. Whenever Nia started to sneak off to investigate the thumping and bumping sounds, Marcus asked what color ear bows she had for Phooey. Unfortunately, Nia took these questions as enthusiasm for the project.

"I'm so glad one of you boys understands that your puppy is definitely going to need some girl time. Tell Conner hi and that if he messes up our doggy salon, I'll publicly humiliate him on the paintball field!" Nia gave a beatific smile.

Somehow, he managed to usher Nia and her mom out of the house. Marcus shut the door and slumped against the other side. They weren't prepared to host Nia's grandma. Not only did he know nothing about interior design, the squirrel could break into the living room at any moment. How could he stop Nia from bringing over additional family members and accosting their dog with hair bows?

As important as those questions were, Marcus didn't have time to consider them further. As soon as he set Phooey down in the hall, she disappeared in a mad sprint away from their resident squirrel.

Rasputin and Phooey kept all three humans charging about the house, all day long. An entire day of near misses thundered by before Marcus heard a faint howl from the garage.

He bolted through the kitchen, practically smashed through the door, and arrived just in time to stumble forward and snatch Phooey out of the air. Marcus clutched their trembling pup to his chest and scanned the garage.

How had she climbed high enough to fall like that?

Several storage tubs lay open. A trail of pillows led from the tubs to a monstrous pile of pillows in the corner. The top of the pillow mountain hovered near the tallest shelf at the back of the garage. Surely Phooey hadn't done all this trying to get something off the shelf. Dogs were smart, but construction projects of this magnitude . . . It wasn't possible.

A china teacup wrapped in tissue had landed on the giant mountain of pillows. It tumbled down and rolled to a stop at Marcus's feet. Why? Why climb the pillows? Marcus squeezed Phooey tight, feeling like he was going to puke. He took three deep breaths and forced thoughts of Conner's accident away.

They'd almost lost her, and for what? If she'd landed wrong . . .

"A fancy teacup!" Conner scooped up the cup and tore off the tissue paper. Then he zoomed toward the kitchen sink.

"You don't suppose . . . " Marcus glanced down at Phooey as he followed Conner into the kitchen. Her tail wagged faster and faster.

Conner filled the cup with cool, crisp water and set it on the floor mat.

Marcus slowly released their bedraggled pup. She gave him a slurp and trundled over to the teacup. Phooey plunged her snout inside and drank and drank and drank.

Finally!

Marcus filled her cup several times.

The kitchen was peaceful for a moment as Phooey plopped down, stared up at the boys, and wagged her tail as fast as a tail could wag. There it was—peace. Perfect peace. A quiet pause in the chaos. A moment with their new dog. Conner wasn't breaking any bones. Marcus wasn't biting his fingernails. Phooey was so adorable he could barely believe she was real.

Conner grinned.

Marcus patted Phooey's fluffy head and dug around in his pocket for one of the dog cookies Aunt Stella had bought before the squirrel rampage really kicked off. Phooey was such a good girl she deserved—

A scratching from above sucked every speck of peace from the room, like Dad's shop vac destroying cobwebs. Everyone looked up. No squirrel. But the skittering sounds continued overhead.

"What's that?" Marcus pointed at a teeny tiny shadow on the ceiling. Or was it a hole?

"He couldn't have, right?" Conner grabbed a broom and gave the ceiling a swift jab.

The broom sank into the ceiling with a crunch.

Conner stared, then oh-so-slowly pulled the broom free.

Sheetrock dust and bits of insulation sifted down.

Silence followed . . . and the squirrel followed shortly after.

Like an angel of destruction, Rasputin burst out of that small hole he'd chewed in the ceiling in a leap both graceful and sure. The attacking rodent bounced off Phooey's back, darted across Conner's chair, bounded onto Marcus's shoulder, and then skittered down and away, taking the cookie in Marcus's hand with him.

Game on!

The chase seemed to last for years. Things broke, items were scattered, one unlucky chair cushion exploded stuffing across the kitchen floor in a horrifying display of decorative death. Marcus mopped up more puppy puddles as terror made all thoughts of potty training evaporate out of Phooey's mind.

Finally, just like a hound dog chasing a racoon, the squirrel treed Phooey.

Rasputin chased her up onto an antique stool in their parents' bathroom, to the laundry basket, and into the white pedestal sink where Phooey was well and truly trapped. Then the little brown beast darted into the closet and was gone, leaving Phooey howling.

Marcus sagged in the doorway. It was all just so exhausting. His feet hurt from chasing Phooey around the house. His ears hurt from Rasputin's angry chitters and all of Phooey's howling. He was even getting dishpan hands from cleaning up so many puppy puddles. Adding a puppy to the home was supposed to rid them of the squirrel, bring incalculable joy, soothe his brother's competitive edge, and ease his parents' stress. Instead, Phooey had stirred the squirrel to increased mayhem and added doggy puddles and hair into the mix. Where was that wretched squirrel, anyway?

Conner wheeled up behind Marcus, giving him a pat on the shoulder. "Here, let me get her. You help Aunt Stella."

Marcus hesitated.

Conner drove to the low bathroom sink and gently turned on the warm water. He got some bubbles worked into Phooey's fur and began the slow process of washing the urine, flour, and something that might have been chewing gum out of her glossy black coat.

Marcus sighed. "OK, call me if you need extra towels or anything." Conner nodded and Marcus left the room, jogging toward the kitchen where their aunt was muttering unfavorable descriptions of squirrels under her breath as she cleaned.

By the time his brother called for him, it was bedtime and the house was a bit cleaner, though not yet returned to its pre-squirrel state. Marcus wrapped a soaked Phooey into a big, fluffy towel and followed Conner to their room. His brother parked his chair and used the loops on the underside of their bunk to get himself to bed. Marcus set Phooey on the floor and got Conner tucked in. Phooey sat in the hall, cringing whenever a pot banged from the kitchen where Aunt Stella was still cleaning fiercely.

"Would you cover up my chair?" Conner asked. Marcus nodded and threw a blanket over the wheelchair.

"I threw the CDs the dog breeder packed for Phooey into our trash," Conner said. "But the one with the nun singing about deer and jam on bread wasn't that bad. Maybe it will help her settle. She's had a rough day."

They'd all had a rough day. Marcus and Conner looked over at Phooey where she sat all soggy and exhausted in the hall. She was still too jumpy to sleep, though, and just as her snout would start to droop down and settle on her paws, a thump or bump or ominous scratching sound would make her jerk awake and start to tremble. Marcus dug a CD out of the trash and put it on.

Phooey pricked her ears and softly padded into the room.

Conner patted his bed.

Phooey stared at him for a long moment. Then she backed up, steeled herself, and made a running leap for a spot next to Conner.

Only half of her made it, leaving her hind legs and floppy tail dangling off the edge. Marcus scooped her up and settled their pup onto a towel. Phooey turned in a circle three times then plopped against Conner's side.

"So," Marcus stroked Phooey's soft coat while Conner gently tugged her ears. "I think Phooey needs a big victory to help overcome her fears."

Conner looked down at Phooey. He framed her squishy puppy face in his hands and whispered. "You can do it, girl. Go, fight, win!"

Phooey wagged and then hid her snout under Conner's blanket.

"She still seems pretty scared," Conner said. How can we help her get a big 'victory' if she's too afraid to even step on the shiny floor in the kitchen?"

"Do you remember the cartoon we watched right before we got Phooey?"

"Yeah, the one where the teenagers and their 'fraidy dog solved mysteries and I was wondering if our dog would solve mysteries . . . But Rasputin isn't a mystery. We know exactly where all the messes are coming from."

"They didn't just solve mysteries, they also made traps. Why waste all our energy chasing the squirrel when we could simply trap the tiny villain? Trap-building is very similar to constructing a Rube Goldberg machine. Nia's an expert at those. At least . . . she's built two, for sure. We can totally do this and Phooey is going to help us, just like that cartoon dog."

"Yeah," Conner said, "their dog trapped that jewel thief in the Sasquatch suit. Phooey isn't any more scaredy than him!"

Marcus carefully kept himself from pointing out that Phooey was a real dog and the animal they were basing their strategy on had been drawn by a cartoonist in the 1960s. Despite the made-up nature of that other dog, this plan just might work. Perhaps Phooey's skillset was less "destroying thieving rodents" and more in line with "chasing marauding critters into traps."

"She could even be part of the trap," Marcus said. Remember Rube Goldberg's parrot?"

Conner's eyes grew wide. He smiled and gave Phooey a hopeful pat.

"Exactly," Marcus said. "I watched a video about it, and Rube Goldberg invented machines that used parrots eating crackers and cats inexplicably balanced on towers of dirty dishes. Why not use Phooey to catch the squirrel?"

Conner scooped Phooey up and made her punch the air with her front paws in victory. "If she did that, Phooey will feel so proud she wouldn't be afraid of anything ever again!"

Phooey slobbered his chin and snuggled closer. She seemed to love the idea.

Marcus grabbed his small notebook and yanked the pencil from under his shoelaces to double check. He wrote: *Perils of Using Phooey in a Rube Goldberg Machine: 1) Phooey becomes even more afraid.* Probably not possible. *2) Phooey messes it up.* Possible but not exactly dangerous. *3) We catch the house on fire with a candle.* It could be a very small candle and they could keep a big glass of water nearby. *4) Nia brings pink clothing that everyone is required to wear in order to have her help.* He and Conner should have their own cool costumes so she wasn't tempted. *5) We catch Aunt Stella instead of the squirrel.* Not likely, since Aunt Stella has been so distracted with cleaning that she probably wouldn't even notice them.

Marcus gave Phooey one last pat before climbing the ladder up to his bunk. He could hear his brother start to snore and Phooey's happy sniffing as she cleaned up the crumbs from Conner's bedtime snack. Marcus glanced around the darkened room. He was glad Conner and Phooey were both too tired to hear the ominous scratching sounds coming from behind the walls.

Where exactly the squirrel had gone was a mystery, but the destructive creature wasn't done yet. Every few minutes, Marcus was startled awake by the skittering of tiny feet and the scratch of small claws somewhere in the darkness beyond.

CHAPTER ELEVEN
Rube Goldberg Machine

The gentle tones of the singing nun CD did not soothe the squirrel. Phooey was well-rested but not any braver come morning, and Rasputin was still going strong. Marcus stumbled into the kitchen hoping for a squirrel-free breakfast.

Sadly, it was not to be.

Aunt Stella nearly bowled him over near the door. She charged after Rasputin, smacking a broom just behind the creature as he darted off, toting a half-eaten toaster pastry.

After a hastily eaten breakfast wedged in the corner of the kitchen where they wouldn't be run over (by either the squirrel or Aunt Stella), the boys put in a call to Nia, their local Rube Goldberg machine expert.

"Absolutely!" was her answer to Marcus's cautious request for her help with a squirrel trap. "You can never have too many Rube Goldberg machines, and Phooey is going to love being the star!"

Marcus was not certain that her statement was true, but he still took down her list of items to find while she finished her chores.

While Marcus grabbed a tealight candle and some twine, Conner shouted from their room. "Rasputin, you're roast-meat for worms!"

Marcus sprinted down the hall and arrived in time to see Conner cradling his new paintball mask and three empty bags of brand-new paintballs.

"Why would a squirrel steal paintballs?" Conner said.

A jagged row of small tooth marks ran along the edge of the new mask. Conner nodded his chin at the box that now only contained a lone bag of paintballs, the limp bags that Rasputin had emptied, and several little pellets of squirrel poo.

"If Rasputin expects them to taste like nuts when he digs them up this winter," Marcus said, "he's in for a disappointment." Despite the image of a hungry Rasputin forlornly nibbling on a florescent green paintball on a snowy day, Marcus didn't feel overly sympathetic.

The boys put off all further dog training to enact a massive anti-squirrel campaign. Rasputin had to go and Phooey was going to help them rid the house of that rotten squirrel once and for all!

Marcus sent Conner after walnuts, marbles both wooden and glass, paintballs, matches, Conner's giant one-pound jawbreaker, toy cars and tracks, dominoes, and a spiral slide for marbles.

Marcus rushed to the kitchen for paper towel tubes, a funnel, peanut butter, a roll of tape, and a large roasting pan.

Once Conner rolled up with the last of their squirrel-trapping gear, Marcus spread everything out on the kitchen floor.

A wild pounding on the door and a shout heralded Nia's arrival.

The three kids gathered around the loose materials. Marcus scribbled a few more possible dangers in his notebook, Conner gave Nia a high five, and Nia snapped her mad-scientist goggles in place and shrugged into a real lab coat.

She dug in her backpack and came up with even more lab coats, including a tiny one for Phooey. What did Nia think they needed lab coats for? They weren't going to spill acid or anything . . . were they?

Still, Marcus accepted his lab coat with a solemn nod. Of course, they should dress for the project. This was serious business.

Conner turned his into a cape.

Phooey wagged and waddled up to greet Nia.

"Oh, she doesn't want a lab coat," Marcus said.

Phooey wagged and sat, calmly accepting a lab coat from their neighbor and even giving her a friendly slurp after being stuffed into the piece of restrictive clothing.

Then their pup noticed the slick flooring, and cringed, scrambling back. Marcus spread out a fluffy towel near all their gear. She padded forward, gave a cautious sniff, and then stretched out on the towel with a happy sigh.

With their Rube Goldberg machine-making attire complete, Nia slammed a set of blueprints down on the floor and spread out the plans for their trap.

The squirrel seemed drawn to the kitchen with its wide variety of food items. Thus, the kitchen and all of its delicacies would become Rasputin's doom.

While Nia and Marcus started construction, Conner worked on Phooey's first command.

It was slow-going. Conner would say, "Sit!" in a firm voice and slowly raise a dog cookie high in the air. As Phooey followed it with her eyes, she would raise her chin and lower her rump until the cookie was so high that she couldn't tip her head back far enough to gaze at it without sitting. Once that rump plopped down, Conner tossed her the cookie and praised her with massive amounts of enthusiasm. They did it over and over and over, but Phooey only performed if there was a cookie involved.

While Conner waved around dog treats, Nia taped a small cardboard platform to the side of the two-tiered cabinet island in the center of the kitchen.

Marcus used sandpaper to create a small divot in the cardboard where the wooden marble would rest. Between attempts to get Phooey to sit, Conner handed him the spiral marble slide and he connected that to the edge of his platform, sanding just a little so that a smooth groove led from the marble's resting place to the slide.

At the bottom of the slide, Nia set up a row of dominoes. Marcus rifled through their box of cars until he found a blue SUV that went fast and had enough weight to shove over the cardboard tube they propped up at the bottom of the car ramp.

Next, Nia filled the matchbox with an assortment of glass and agate marbles.

Marcus balanced the box of marbles on top of the cardboard tube. Marcus tore off strip after strip of tape, and Nia used it to secure a small plastic funnel just below the precariously positioned box of marbles. Using even more tape, she placed a paper towel tube at an angle below the funnel spout.

"OK," Nia said, "I need a car with a wide base and free-moving wheels. It should be big enough to stick a candle on top."

Marcus searched through their box until he came up with an alien spaceship car with a wide, flat top and monster wheels.

"Perfect." Nia stuck a wad of tape to the bottom of a tealight candle and smooshed it into place on top of the car. Then she placed the car and candle at the base of the paper towel tube where the marbles would tumble out and push the small vehicle forward.

Now for the finale. This part actually had neon lightning bolts around it in the blueprints and *Finale!!!* written in sparkly purple. Nia got a chair and the roll of heavy twine. She tied the twine around the middle of the roasting pan to form a kind of belt. Then she tied four short strands to the twine. Next, she tied these four strands to a really long strand so that the huge pan could hang steady in the air. Nia looped the long strand through a plant hook on the ceiling. Both Nia and Marcus pulled on the long strand until the pan rose into the air, swaying gently on the end of the twine. Once it was in position, she tied the string off to the leg of a stool, being careful to position the twine so that the candle flame would be right under it when the marbles made the alien car roll forward.

"Do you need the walnuts?" Conner asked, holding up an entire bag.

Nia scanned their creation. "Oh, yeah! Let's bait the trap."

Scattering cracked walnuts and paintballs smeared in peanut butter beneath the hanging roast pan took just a moment. Nia carefully lit the candle, sat back, and . . . well, sat and sat and continued to sit.

The only sounds were of Phooey gnawing on a new bone, Aunt Stella sternly vacuuming up the bag of sunflower seeds that Rasputin had scattered across the guestroom carpet, and the skittering scratches of squirrely feet as the small invader rampaged throughout the rest of the house.

Except for Mom's showroom.

Thankfully, Marcus had managed to keep the sliding door shut all day. But even with access to the living room denied, Rasputin did not venture into the kitchen.

While Nia bedazzled Phooey's tiny lab coat with sequins and chicken feathers dyed purple, the boys took turns holding the giant jawbreaker at the ready. First Conner and then Marcus, then Conner again while Marcus made sandwiches, then Marcus while Conner ate, and finally back to Conner. It was incredibly boring.

Marcus replaced the tealight with a fresh candle. He designed a new card for their Puppy Panic game: Roving Squirrel Beast. If the card was placed into play, the puppy character either gained two obedience points (if her obedience was above three) or lost two obedience (if her obedience was under three). The flavor text read, "Small but mighty, the Roving Squirrel Beast reveals what lies within a young warrior's heart." After staring at the card a moment, Marcus glanced at Phooey. Did their pup have a streak of bravery, somewhere deep-deep-deep inside? Or had Marcus chosen the most fainthearted pup in the entire litter for his bold and adventurous brother?

Conner gasped.

Nia gave a tiny squeak.

Marcus turned and saw they were both holding their breath, pointing at the doorway.

With a flash of brown, their own Roving Squirrel Beast darted into the room. Rasputin started to climb the kitchen drawer knobs but paused halfway up the cabinets. He leapt down, flew across the linoleum, and skidded to a stop at the pile of walnuts.

Ever so slowly, Conner raised the giant jawbreaker.

Phooey's head snapped up. She stared at the jawbreaker, eyes intent. A string of drool dangled from her jowl. Phooey's tail beat the air with a wild wag that sent the wooden marble rolling across the cardboard platform, down the groove, and into the spiral slide. The marble hit the dominoes. The dominoes pushed the toy car down the ramp. The car toppled the cardboard tube, spilling the matchbox full of glass and agate marbles. The marbles showered down, making a deafening noise in the silent room. Some entered the mouth of the funnel and some glanced off, clattering to the floor below.

At the sudden noise, Phooey sprang to her feet, dropping her bone.

A few of the marbles spiraled through the funnel and down the paper towel tube.

Not knowing where the scary noise had come from, Phooey scrambled in a circle, slipping and sliding on the smooth linoleum, yipping out cries for help.

Her howling spooked Rasputin.

The marbles hit the car with the lit candle on top.

The squirrel darted away from the bait, rushing straight toward Phooey.

The car and candle rolled forward and lurched to a stop beneath the twine.

Phooey scrambled away when she saw the fierce squirrel approaching. She cut hard to the side in an attempt to turn. Instead of halting, her efforts sent her into a smooth slide across the floor. She bounced off the front of the stove and ricocheted back toward the boys.

The flame burned through the string.

Phooey skidded into the pile of bait, sending walnuts and paintballs flying.

The roasting pan descended.

Rasputin gave an angry, chittering cry and darted away.

Thump! The roast pan landed in the middle of the kitchen floor.

Phooey disappeared, trapped. Their big pup was completely engulfed by the massive pan.

They sat in stunned silence.

It wasn't silent for long. A mournful howl echoed from under the pan, followed by a sad little whine. The boys lunged forward to save their poor, trapped pup. Nia chased the squirrel with her clothing bedazzler.

When Marcus pulled off the pan, Phooey sneezed once and then bolted from the room with her tail between her legs. She left a puddle behind. But some way, somehow, she managed to take Conner's giant jawbreaker with her into hiding.

Marcus didn't even chase her. He flopped back onto the linoleum and stared up at the ceiling. A Rube Goldberg machine had been their very best plan. He'd sought help, given his all, done everything he thought he could accomplish and then some.

It had not been enough.

Phooey's distant howls grew muffled as she hid underneath something to whimper and cry. Marcus wondered if there was room in there for him, too.

CHAPTER TWELVE
Phooey Loves China Teacups More Than Boxing

That night, Phooey was so exhausted she fell asleep before Marcus could lug her into their room. Just because their pup was unconscious didn't mean she was any easier to carry. In fact, her limp body kept sagging and almost slipping out of his tired arms. Once he got her heaved onto the mattress next to Conner, Marcus flopped across the foot of his brother's bed and sighed.

"I've got a new plan for training her," he vaguely pointed in Phooey's direction, "so Mom won't notice her size and . . . everything."

Conner raised a brow at Marcus's words, but didn't say anything. He just leaned closer to their pup and ran his fingers through Phooey's soft coat.

Marcus didn't wait to hear whatever doubts his brother had, and pressed on. "I was reading earlier, and all the books say you need to socialize young puppies so they're not afraid of new things."

"What do you mean, socialize her?"

"We need to show her new stuff while making her feel safe. The books suggested taking puppies to the park and on buses and letting them hear loud noises while they're held close in your arms."

"We socialized her to squirrels all day long." Conner glanced at Phooey as she gave a shuddering sigh and burrowed deeper into his blankets.

"But she didn't feel safe. Maybe we could have caught her and snuggled her while Aunt Stella chased the squirrel with her broom."

"Yeah, getting attacked by the squirrel didn't help. Getting caught in our trap didn't help, either. So, do we need to get her out where she will see that squirrels are just big wimps and wheelchairs aren't monsters?" Conner asked.

"Exactly."

"She looked really scared. We have a lot of work to do if she thinks squirrels are the most terrifying animals in the neighborhood. Wait till she catches sight of those llamas at the junk shop." Conner sighed and went back to petting Phooey. Then he froze, mid-pat. "This is just like that old boxing movie! We're training Phooey, right?"

"Yeah." Marcus frowned. Conner didn't expect Phooey to fight the llamas, did he? It was a step down from fighting bears, but was probably a really bad idea, what with her squirrel phobia and all.

"She just needs a training sequence, like the movie. We'll put on some loud music about tigers, give her raw eggs to drink, and then make her run up and down the basement stairs a lot. After that, she faces the squirrel in a bout to the death and learns to pull my wheelchair like a Roman chariot!"

"Uh . . ." Marcus wondered if perhaps Conner was a bit too enthusiastic about dog training. Wait, who was he kidding? Conner was too enthusiastic about absolutely everything. "We're not supposed to go near the basement. Stairs, you know. Let's start with something less terrifying, like a stuffed squirrel or maybe a toy wheelchair with lunch meat on it."

"Chemical-free lunch meat." Conner smiled down at Phooey as he said it.

"Yes," Marcus gave her big snout a quick kiss and ruffled her ears. "Chemical-free lunch meat wrapped around a very small, very ordinary toy wheelchair. I think Nia has one for her dolls. We'll work up from there."

Marcus stroked Phooey's soft fur while his brother and pup drifted off to sleep. He pulled out his notebook and tugged the pencil from under his shoelaces. He wrote: *Perils of Boxing-Style Training Sequence for a Dog: 1) Dog actually learns how to box and is confiscated by the government for testing.* Not likely. *2) Conner learns how to box and terrorizes the neighborhood with this new skill.* Conner is already terrorizing the neighborhood. *3) One of us falls down the stairs during training.* This is a real concern.

But, if they were careful, Marcus was pretty sure that Conner's plan wouldn't make Phooey any more afraid than she already was. And, who knew, it might actually help!

The next day, the boys ignored Rasputin's rampaging and focused on their pup's training. It was already Tuesday morning. They didn't have school because of spring break, but Mom and Dad would be home tomorrow. Phooey wasn't quite ready to impress.

She needed to be well-trained.

So well-trained that eighteen extra pounds of puppy wouldn't bother Mom.

Marcus had gotten a little bit of sleep, but the ominous scritching and scratching that came from behind the walls still woke him several times. Both Conner and Phooey also appeared bleary, but they didn't have time for napping. Their puppy desperately needed both training and socialization.

Marcus stumbled through the house, groggy, blinking his eyes to keep them open and trying to find items that were new to Phooey, but not too terrifying.

First, he coaxed her toward a houseplant by trying to feed her little round slices of hot dog.

Phooey turned up her nose.

Conner dug through the fridge for Dad's super-healthy, organic, all-chicken sausage.

Phooey was inspired by the sausage and inched closer to the plant. Their giant pup cautiously sniffed one shiny leaf before yelping and leaping back.

Conner zipped around in his wheelchair, grabbing things that were a little scarier: the blender, Dad's electric razor, a cake mixer, and Mom's creepy collection of ceramic pigs. These were for later, once Phooey had conquered her fear of the toy wheelchair Marcus had borrowed from Nia.

Phooey found an item of her own: one of the TP-cover dolls that Aunt Stella had purchased from Nia's mom. A pink one, not green. Phooey pranced out of the bathroom with the TP doll gripped in her jaws, wagging her tail and holding her head at a jaunty angle. At least she wasn't afraid of TP, crocheted dresses, or dolls. That was something, right?

Marcus glanced over his shoulder to where his brother was making her a little gray sweatshirt out of old teddy bear clothes. Conner's fierce dog couldn't tote around a TP doll.

Marcus pointed theatrically toward the kitchen. "Oh, Phooey! Who will eat all those unclaimed cookies?"

The giant pup trundled off to investigate a bag of gingersnaps Rasputin had scattered. She hopped across the shiny floor on the dish towels they'd used to clean up all of the terrible squirrel messes. Marcus snatched up the doll and plonked it back onto the spare toilet paper roll in the bathroom.

Phooey bounded back, munching treats and looking for her doll. She sniffed the spot on the floor where she'd dropped it. Then she followed the exact path Marcus had walked, wagging her tail and crunching on the cookies. When she reached the closed bathroom door, Phooey looked up at Marcus, then turned and booped the door with her nose.

"No, girl. How about this?" He handed her a squeaky chicken. Phooey darted behind his legs and growled.

He offered her a squeaky spider, toy armadillo, and plush Sasquatch.

Growl. Growl. Growl.

Conner wheeled up. "The boxing movie holds the key! Phooey can't help being brave with a gray sweatshirt and fighting music!"

Marcus nodded and kept his doubts to himself. He found the right playlist and let the inspiring 1970s theme song play over and over. Conner had already gotten out the stuff for her "fear-banishing smoothie." Eggs, spinach, and his secret ingredient, which turned out to be a bag of pepperoni slices.

Marcus fired up the blender and mixed Phooey's power drink.

Phooey ran.

Oh, yeah. The blender was one of her "scary things." Marcus gave Conner a handful of pepperoni slices for luring their pup back into the kitchen for her smoothie.

Hmmm . . . the discouraged boxer in the movie had simply chugged a glass of eggs, but Phooey was a little daintier. What would make the drink extra special for their "little" girl doggy?

Conner pointed at a camouflage coffee mug. Marcus poured the drink into it and set it on the floor.

Phooey sniffed. Her tail beat out a happy rhythm. She reached out one front paw, placed it on the linoleum, and then jerked it back with a yelp.

She sat on the floor mat where the kitchen met the hall and gave them a determined look that seemed to say, "Are you kidding me? I can't walk on that!" Marcus scooted the drink over to the very edge of the kitchen. Phooey gave a cautious sniff, started toward the drink, and then recoiled. Was she looking at the mug? Surely not.

They tried a cup from Yellowstone National Park that had roaring grizzly bears, a race car mug, and finally the "World's Greatest Dad" mug that had a stack of pancakes and a man in pajama pants and a chef's hat. Phooey turned up her nose at each and every one.

Marcus tried one more cup. The one Phooey had found during her perilous fall off the pillow mountain in the garage. Grandma's real china teacup with the 14-carat gold rim and rosebud design. He poured the power drink into the dainty cup, set it in the matching saucer, and placed the offering before Phooey.

Her tail whirled in a circle and she gave a bright bark before plunging her snout into the fragile cup and slurping down the drink.

OK, then. To the basement for stair climbing.

In the boxing movie, the uninspired boxer had overcome all his weaknesses by climbing stairs in a gray sweatshirt and shouting victoriously at the top. Phooey had the invigorating music and had slurped down her drink of eggs. All she had left were the sweatshirt and the stairs.

The family had moved to a variety of virtually stair-free houses after Conner's accident. But the shag-carpeted basement did have ten shaggy steps that descended into Dad's "man cave" where he stored stacks of board games, all of the tools owned by their great-grandfathers, and an old weightlifting set. Conner stuffed the teddy bear sweatshirt over Phooey's fuzzy head.

She growled and bit at the sleeves, thrashing in a wild circle.

Marcus eyed her cautiously, noting her angry attack upon the adorable clothing. With some trepidation he seized their sweatshirted pup. She stopped growling and gave him some cheery slurps and tail wags. Fending off her slobbery affection, Marcus toted Phooey to the bottom of the stairs and sat on the bottom step.

The boxing music blared.

"OK, you need to make her front paws punch at the air, like this." From the top of the stairs, Conner gave a demonstration of fierce punches that matched the music precisely. Marcus looked down at Phooey. She scratched her ear with a back paw and met his gaze with soulful eyes.

"Phooey, sit!" Marcus commanded.

Phooey bounced up and slurped his chin. He plopped her in his lap and held up her paws to make a few punches.

She slurped his ear and wagged.

Punches complete, it was now time for the stairs. Marcus set Phooey's front paws on the first step. She just stood there. He gave her a gentle push. She sat. He pulled her into a stand and forced her up the first step. She slurped his hands and plopped her furry rump down the minute he let go.

Phooey Kerflooey

"Come on, Marcus. She's got to train and get brave."

With the music blaring, Marcus nodded up at Conner and grabbed Phooey around her chubby tummy. He lugged their reluctant pup up and down the stairs himself.

Her four paws hung limp, dragging along the stairs. Her tail kept time to the music though: *wag wag waaaag, wag wag waaaaag, wag wag waaaaag, wag wag waaaaaag.*

Conner peered down at their progress. "Mom is counting on her guarding the decorator stuff from the squirrel. If she doesn't start battling Rasputin today, I'll have to break my other leg to convince Mom to let us keep her." Conner's expression grew contemplative in a way that sent Marcus's heart rate into overdrive. "I bet if I needed her furry powers to help me recover, Mom wouldn't take Phooey back even if she doesn't fight the squirrel right away." A huge smile broke across Conner's face.

Marcus gulped at the sight, clutching Phooey to his chest as he paused to bring a bit of sanity back to their training session.

"No, you just got out of your cast." Marcus leaned against the basement wall and squinted up at Conner. *Please, please be careful.* His brother's chair was really close to the stairs. Marcus should have listed *purposely broken limbs* as a danger in his notebook before they started mixing up Phooey's eggs. "Why don't you scoot back a little?"

Phooey gave a little yip. Marcus glanced down and realized that he had squeezed her tight as he stared up at his daredevil brother. If Conner was desperate to keep Phooey, would he resort to plunging down the steps to his doom? This was just like the "half-pipe incident" two months ago at the skate park with Adam Weisburn.

"She's doing great, Conner. Look at her tail."

Phooey wagged obligingly.

Conner rolled even closer to the edge to look at Phooey's wagging.

"See," Marcus shouted up the stairs as he continued to haul their huge, fuzzy girl up and down and up and down. "Braver all ready. You can call off the stair-surfing and scoot back now." Marcus hoisted Phooey up for Conner to see and she slurped the air in

Conner's direction, as though assuring him of her sudden bravery.

Conner did not scoot back.

When "they," meaning Marcus, had done the stairs ten times, he collapsed at the top. Phooey plopped down on his chest and promptly fell asleep. "OK," he mumbled. "I think she is about as inspired as I can make her."

Conner rolled off to grab more dog treats.

Marcus stretched and rubbed his aching back.

Phooey snored.

Her first post-training-sequence socialization challenge: the linoleum floor in the kitchen.

Mom's old Corgi had been trained to only walk on hard floors. According to her, she'd never found a dog hair in her soup or gotten drool on her clothes, all because of this simple rule. The only problem: according to Phooey, linoleum was public enemy #1. Well, maybe enemy #2 right after Rasputin. How could Phooey impress Mom if she wouldn't even step on the kind of flooring she was supposed to stay on all the time?

Marcus set Phooey down in the kitchen. She bounded away in great desperate leaps, trying to keep her paws from touching the horrifying floor. After ten tries, she ran away and then pranced back with the TP doll held firmly in her jaws.

Marcus bent and snatched the TP doll away.

Phooey howled.

"Why don't you start with the cotton balls?" Conner asked from around the corner, where he was blocking Phooey's escape route with his wheelchair.

"What if she hates tape, too?"

"It doesn't hurt to try, right?"

"It could make her even more scared," Marcus muttered. Conner didn't reply. After a long silence, Marcus used a rolled-up piece of painter's tape to stick a wad of cotton on Phooey's front paw. She shook her paw and nipped at the cotton while he quickly taped the other three. Marcus set Phooey onto the kitchen floor. She bounded high and galloped to the carpet before pausing to tear off the cotton balls and chew on the tape.

"Careful, she's going to choke." Conner pointed from around the corner as Phooey tried to down an entire cotton ball.

Marcus confiscated all the tape and cotton balls before she ate any. Although, hadn't there been four wads of tape?

Next, Marcus put a silicone potholder underneath each of Phooey's paws. The irony did not escape him. This was just like that ridiculous card in his Puppy Panic game. The one he'd thought was so unrealistic, because why on earth would a real dog need a bridge of potholders just to walk across a floor? Phooey stood still, staring at the colorful squares of non-skid material. She wagged and gave a happy yip. Perfect. The only problem: she wouldn't move off the potholders. What good was a dog who was stuck in one spot all the time?

Conner grabbed more potholders and a few hand towels out of the drawer and tossed them to Marcus. Marcus scattered them all over the scary linoleum. Phooey approved. She pranced across the kitchen, leaping from potholder to towel to washrag to napkin.

The doorbell rang.

Phooey forgot all her bravery lessons and bolted toward the living room. Not seeing the closed door in time, she bonked her snout on the wooden slider. She stared at the door for a moment, an upset tilt to her ears. Then she galloped down the hall and flattened herself out on the carpet to wriggle underneath Conner's bed. From the safety of her bunk-bed cave, their brave dog howled and howled and howled.

Marcus opened the slider, stomped through the living room, and yanked open the front door.

Nia stared back at him, sparkling.

Marcus blinked. So bright.

She wore a purple tutu over her jeans, had brushed more glitter across her cheeks, and replaced the pink beads in her braids with sparkly purple ones. Nia and all her sparkles listened to the howling for a moment. "Phooey?"

"Yep." Marcus said.

"Well . . . I brought her a present. I thought you guys might be a bit short on the essentials." Nia held up a pink baggy from the hair accessory store at the mall.

Oh, great. Conner was going to love this. It was bad enough that Nia could beat him at paintball, but hair bows for their huge and fierce puppy? That was uncalled for. "Thanks. I'm sure she'll love them." Marcus didn't want to be rude. Was there a polite way to refuse hair accessories?

"Can I say hi?"

"Sure." Marcus steeled himself. It was a little embarrassing that their awesome new dog was hiding under the bed instead of barking at strangers and chasing off deadly squirrels. But she was fuzzy and big and adorable. Maybe Nia would remember those things, instead.

Marcus led the way through the perfect living room, snapped the slider shut, and hustled Nia down the hall before she had too much time to wonder at the tragic state of the kitchen. Marcus threw away a few noodle wrappers Rasputin had dragged down the hall while Nia peeked into their bedroom, looking around for Phooey.

"What's wrong? She seems scared."

"Yeah, the doorbell."

Phooey Kerflooey

Nia flopped onto the carpet in front of the bed and gently reached out to stroke Phooey's soft fur. The big pup wriggled out of her hiding place and bounced in lopsided circles around their neighbor. When Nia sat up, Phooey plopped in her lap, tail wagging out a steady rhythm. "What a beauty."

Phooey gave a doggy grin at Nia's words and her tail wagged into overdrive.

"You picked a great dog, Marcus. She's so sweet and gentle."

Marcus smiled. Phooey was beautiful and gentle. Especially for such a big dog.

"Where's Conner?" Nia asked.

Marcus's smile evaporated. "She's afraid of his chair, too."

Nia bent down and Phooey washed her face with puppy kisses. "That's no good. They should bond." Nia pulled a huge bow out of her bag. She gathered the fluff above Phooey's ear and clipped the bow on.

"She's afraid of toothbrushes and linoleum. I don't think a bow is a good idea."

"Just look at her! She loves it."

Marcus glanced at Phooey. Was she sitting taller? Had her ears always sat at that jaunty angle? Could she possibly be feeling . . . brave?

"Hey, Conner," Nia called. "Roll in here. Let's see what she does."

Conner eased around the corner.

Phooey wagged.

Conner rolled into the bedroom, closer and closer until he stopped right in front of the bunk bed. Phooey bounded over to the wheelchair and plopped her front paws on his knees. Conner beamed, scratching her silky ears and smoothing the soft fur on her back.

"Now, you said she's not sleeping." Nia said in a matter-of-fact tone. "We just have to find something soothing that you guys don't have to stay awake for. Something like music or a whooshy fan."

Marcus looked at his brother. A fan was a good idea.

Conner was easing the bow out of Phooey's hair, scratching her ear while he did it, trying to distract her.

As soon as the bow slid free, Phooey launched herself from his lap. She pounded across the floor and wriggled beneath the bed like the world's fattest caterpillar.

"Look, her bow just came free. That's all." Nia picked up the bow and looked under the bed. "Here you go, girl."

Bow in place, Phooey pranced back over to Conner and leaned against his knee. Conner scowled, but didn't remove it again.

Phooey wouldn't nap to a fan, or rainforest sounds, or Christmas carols. But she absolutely loved Nia's *Princess Music From Around The World* collection.

Conner had wanted their new dog to chase Nia if she brought over her bedazzler, or her music, or her massive collection of dimple-faced baby dolls with their evil plastic smiles. Conner and Nia were best friends, but Conner was much more skeptical of the bedazzler than Nia had been of paintball guns.

Marcus refused to meet Conner's gaze. This was the exact opposite of chasing Nia. Unless you counted chasing Nia in order to get another ear bow.

Phooey loved all of the madness from Nia's bag of horrors. The way she gazed up at Nia with pure adoration, Marcus was pretty sure the only way she'd bite her was if they dumped a truckload of peanut butter over their neighbor's head.

Phooey galloped to retrieve the well-chewed TP doll from the bathroom to drop into Nia's lap. She collapsed to the floor snoring whenever a princess and woodland creature sang a duet. She even crossed the kitchen linoleum unaided after Nia tied a big ribbon onto her tail. Phooey was just like the little elephant who needed his magic feather to fly. Only, Phooey's magic came from frills, sparkles, and Nia. How could their dog like the neighbor more than her own boys?

Phooey suddenly became an obedience prodigy. She stayed for Nia, she came for Nia. She laid down, spun in circles, did an adorable little high five, and even sat for Nia. As long as their beglittered neighbor kept the praise and floofy hair clips coming, Phooey was a puppy genius.

Finally, once Nia had thoroughly corrupted their guard dog, even going so far as to sprinkle glitter in her soft fur, she gave Phooey a goodbye kiss on the snout and headed home.

Phooey Kerflooey

At bedtime, Phooey raced the boys into their room. She galloped around the corner, leapt onto Conner's bed and stretched out as far as her four paws would go so that she filled the entire mattress.

"It's OK," Conner said eyeing the tiny bit of bed that was left. "If you shove me way over into the corner, we'll both fit."

After he fell out of bed trying to leave enough room for the furry cover-hog, Aunt Stella banished Phooey to the laundry room.

Later, when Aunt Stella was snoring with her earplugs firmly in place, Marcus snuck to Phooey's crate. She was crying and pacing and sad. Maybe Nia was right and something special from home would help. Marcus spread the pink blanket that Jessie had sent home with them across the floor and laid the mangled TP doll beside her. Phooey turned in a circle three times and then plopped down, fast asleep.

Marcus tiptoed into the kitchen to look for a snack, preferably something Rasputin had not chewed. He found an apple with no nibbles and was about to turn out the lights when the crying resumed. Marcus ran back to the laundry room.

Phooey was pacing. The blanket and doll were gone. In their place was Conner's favorite blue pillowcase and an action figure who wielded a cutlass and had an angry plastic ferret sitting on his shoulder. The toys were much bolder options, but Phooey did not approve. How had Conner wheeled in here without Marcus noticing?

Phooey nudged the ferret guy away until he was crammed into the corner. Then she crouched and made a big poo, right on top of the ferret. She sat down in the other corner and let out a low, warbling howl.

It was going to be a long, long, super-long night.

CHAPTER THIRTEEN
The Monster's Lair

The next morning, Marcus woke up to find the house sparkle-free. The frilly hair clips had vanished. The bottle of glitter lotion for Phooey's nose was missing. But what sent Phooey into a chorus of warbling howls was the tragic discovery that her TP doll had somehow evaporated into thin air.

Conner didn't say a thing, but both Marcus and Phooey knew who to blame.

And blame him, Phooey did.

She huffed out great sighing breaths whenever Conner rolled into the room. She plopped her chin on her front paws and gave him the full force of her tragically sad puppy eyes. She even tugged on his pant leg until he followed her into the bathroom, where she pointed at the back of the toilet with her snout then glanced back at Conner with eyes full of judgment.

With all her bows and dolls confiscated, Phooey was impossible to train.

Conner wasn't revealing the location of the hidden doll, and they only had two options left before Mom and Dad came home: trap Rasputin the squirrel or face their parents with the hairiest, wimpiest puppy ever to refuse to walk on linoleum.

Their parents were coming home that night. Marcus and Conner had less than twelve hours to both trap Rasputin and inspire Phooey to doggy greatness.

Marcus leaned his head back against the wall and stared at the ceiling. Why did they need a fierce dog in the first place? Phooey was fluffy and cuddly and adorable. In fact, she was actually quite a bit fiercer if she had her doll and a few bows in her fur. What was Conner's problem?

Conner rolled past way too fast and Marcus was reminded exactly what his brother's problem was. Since his accident, only dangerous things seemed to please his little brother. It's like he had to defend his title as "Most Reckless Kid in Town," and prove that the wheelchair was not a setback to all things irresponsible. And it hadn't been. Conner was more irresponsible than ever. But that didn't change the fact that Marcus had let his brother down by not waking up last year when Conner had sneaked out and gotten hurt. No, if Conner needed a fierce dog, Phooey just had to get fierce. That was it—end of story.

OK, new plan.

A simple box trap seemed the best design to fall back on. While Conner wheeled out to the recycle pile to grab four boxes, Marcus scrounged the park for sturdy sticks. Aunt Stella supplied the string, and of course they used paintballs and peanut butter for bait.

First, they found a likely location for each box. Marcus propped each one up with a stick. After tying a string to the stick, the device was ready to trap their squirrel.

The concept was simple. When Rasputin ran underneath the box to nibble at the peanut butter or tote off more paintballs, they'd pull the string. The stick would move. The box would fall. The squirrel would be trapped.

Simple.

Marcus was just setting up his box in their bedroom when he heard Aunt Stella scream. Letting the box crash to the floor, he raced down the hall. Where was she? He blasted into the living room, but the noises were now behind him. Marcus spun and charged back down the hall. There, in Mom and Dad's room.

Aunt Stella stood backed up against the door with a hand over her mouth. She stared at Dad's dresser.

"What happened?" Marcus asked.

She tried to fan herself with a small bag from the jewelry store but gave up when it didn't make any breeze. "I was just looking for a better hiding place for your mother's present. Somewhere safe from Phooey. I was going to tuck it under your dad's socks in his dresser." Aunt Stella slid a small box from the bag and snapped it open. The beautiful ring sparkled in the dim light.

Marcus glanced around the room. What had scared his aunt?

"But what's wrong? You screamed."

"Yes, I opened up your dad's drawer and found that." She pointed toward the dresser with a grimace.

Marcus crept across the blue carpet and climbed up onto his parents' bed. Everything was very tidy and smelled like dried flowers and the cream his dad put on his back after work. He stood, gripping the fancy headboard, and peered into Dad's sock drawer.

Something had moved in.

Old pillow stuffing, torn up socks, and shredded facial tissues were mounded in one corner of the drawer.

A nest. A nest that was overflowing with paintballs.

They had found Rasputin's lair.

The boys set up their traps accordingly. If squirrel-headquarters was Dad's sock drawer, the logical place for traps would be the paths to and from that location. The problem: most of the time, Rasputin appeared to move through the walls.

However, he needed to eat and had to come out sometime. They set up Conner's box at one end of the hall and Aunt Stella's at the other. They made a trap by the bathroom for Phooey. The string to trigger it was tied to her paw. Since she always ran from the squirrel, there was a small chance she might actually catch him as she fled. Marcus set his trap up in the doorway to Dad and Mom's room. Rasputin would have to come home sometime.

Next came the hard part: waiting for their quarry—again.

Squirrels were apparently not very punctual animals. Rasputin didn't scamper past. Rasputin didn't climb the bookshelves. Rasputin didn't even chitter insults at them from the ceiling fan.

Aunt Stella moved her trap to the kitchen and tied the string to her ankle while she started lunch. Conner sat in his chair reading comics and snacking on pistachios. Phooey chewed on a bone, but kept knocking her box over every time she got up to hide her treat under the bathroom mat.

Marcus lay on his stomach in the hall, completely focused on Rasputin's lair. Sure, he'd eaten a PB&J sandwich when Aunt Stella brought one by. But he'd kept his eyes trained on that box during every bite. He didn't read while he waited, like Conner. He didn't sing, like Aunt Stella. He didn't chase his tail, like Phooey. Marcus lay motionless, daring Rasputin to come his way.

Afternoon moseyed by and the shadow made by his mom's potted cactus stretched long across the floor. Dust motes floated in the slant of sunlight that came through the window. Even the birdsong from outside sounded weary. Like the robins and mourning doves were ready to call it a day.

A skittering under the bed sent a jolt through Marcus. Something moved in the deep shadows. Something that hadn't been there before. He held the string steady, not wanting to trip the trap early. The room seemed to freeze for a long, breathless moment. Then Rasputin darted across the floor.

Marcus's hand twitched, but the squirrel wasn't under the box. He scampered up the side of Dad's dresser and dove into the drawer. A flash of fluffy tail was the only clue that the squirrel had passed. A crunching noise filled the silence. Marcus narrowed his eyes. What was that furry beast eating? There wasn't anything to nibble in that drawer except paintballs.

Paintballs!

More crunching. Marcus envisioned the squirrel with blue paint oozing from his jaws. Most paintballs were made with a soap base. Not very tasty. Marcus pictured the painty squirrel frolicking in a pile of rolled up socks and faded tighty-whities. All of Dad's socks were white!

Well, they wouldn't be anymore.

Come on Rasputin, smell the peanut butter. Dash on over to this awesome box.

Marcus's mental urging didn't seem to have any effect. The munching continued. Marcus stared at the dresser. Was that a tail? No, just a shadow. He counted the knots in the pinewood drawers, then followed the patterns made by the grain of the wood.

The swirling knots really drew the eye. Marcus rested his head on the arm that held the string. His whole arm twitched as it began to go numb.

The skittering and scratching all through the night hadn't allowed him enough rest. The long, monotonous day spent staring at traps hadn't helped. Despite the nearness of their nemesis, Marcus's head drooped against his arm. His eyes sagged as the squirrel failed to reappear.

He jerked awake. Yikes, that was close! He propped his head up and rubbed at his face with his free hand.

He listened. No skittering. He glanced at the drawer. It was silent. He let his eyes roam the room. No squirrel on the bed. Nothing darting across the floor. No furry miscreant attacking Mom's dried roses. Nothing by the—

A brown head peered out of the box trap, looked both ways, and then Rasputin made a run for it.

Marcus gritted his teeth. The little beast had been right there, in the trap. Rasputin darted up the dresser drawers like a circus performer and dropped a peanut butter-smeared paintball into the sock drawer.

Phooey Kerflooey

Marcus tightened his hand around the string. This was it. The squirrel knew where the stash was. Now all he had to do was wait.

Rasputin gave a contemptuous chitter and bounded down the dresser knobs. The squirrel sniffed the air, as though he could actually smell Marcus. Maybe Rasputin only came out when it looked like Marcus was falling asleep. Marcus let his head sag, peeking through almost-closed eyes at the box. *Come on, come on.* The squirrel scanned the room for an impossibly long moment, froze with his nose in the air, and then zipped under the box.

Marcus pulled the string.

The box fell.

It twitched and shuddered.

After a hesitant lurch, the entire box trap slid across the room. Rasputin was under the box, but definitely not captured. The box thumped into the wall.

Marcus made a dive. His fingers brushed cardboard. Before he could get a firm grip, the box was off again. Through the door and down the hall.

The box careened down the hallway, faster and faster, bashing into one wall and then another.

"Conner, Aunt Stella, he's going toward the—"

Marcus's toe caught on a stack of dog training books he'd forgotten in the hall, and he stumbled. He landed on hands and knees but kept going. He scrambled forward like Phooey bounding after the TP doll. Marcus grabbed the doorknob to their bedroom and hauled himself up to continue the chase.

Rasputin darted out of the hallway and into the kitchen. The squirrel made a wild circle around the room. Aunt Stella pulled her string and tripped her box trap. In all the excitement, she also dropped a huge bowl full of cornmeal she'd been mixing into cornbread batter. Ironically, her trap tipped forward, clipping the corner of Marcus's box which swerved, hit Aunt Stella's dropped bowl, and lifted clean off the squirrel, allowing Rasputin to dart back into the hall at an unhindered sprint.

He still held a peanut butter paintball in his teeth as he scampered, sending Phooey running.

Phooey Kerflooey

Phooey, disoriented by terror, slammed through the mound of flour and cornmeal which poofed up in a mighty cloud.

The squirrel fled back down the hall and into the boys' room. He bounded on top of Conner's trap and up his arm.

Conner jerked to the side. His wheelchair lurched as Phooey ran by howling. Concern flashed across Conner's face and he hurtled his chair down the hall and after their pup. "Don't let that squirrel scare you, girl." Conner slowed for a moment, as though searching his thoughts. He smiled and took off again at full speed, shouting after the squirrel. "He hast no more brain than I have in mine elbows."

Marcus blinked. How on earth did his brother remember all those Shakespeare quotes?

Phooey did not seem inspired. She darted sideways and ran into the bathroom as Rasputin chattered menacingly.

Conner tried to follow at full speed.

His wheel caught on the frame of the bathroom door as he whizzed by. Conner was wheeling fast—

too fast. The chair snapped to the side, and into the bathroom.

Conner flew out of his seat and into the air.

Phooey tumbled underneath his chair, tail over paws.

Marcus heard a terrible smack, and a thump, followed by sad whines. Phooey limped to the bathroom doorway favoring her right front paw.

He approached slowly and bent to scoop her up. It was quiet in the bathroom. Where was Conner? His brother was never quiet.

Conner's chair lay just inside the doorway, but Conner had kept going. He'd launched through the bathroom door and smacked right into the shiny porcelain toilet.

Marcus froze.

One wheel on Conner's chair spun in a slow circle.

Conner lay still and silent.

Phooey limped first toward Conner and then Marcus, back and forth, unsure.

The squirrel darted up Conner's chair, dropped the paintball onto the upside-down seat, and then leapt over Conner's limp foot and back into the hall towards Mom and Dad's bedroom.

After a horrible moment of complete stillness, Conner groaned and pushed himself up on one elbow. Marcus started forward, but Aunt Stella shoved past him to Conner's side.

"Gracious gophers! Are you all right, honey?" She reached both hands toward him, but stumbled to a stop. She paused for a beat and then slumped sideways into a faint.

Marcus's stomach lurched and a surge of fear tightened his chest. He forced himself to breathe slowly, stepped over his aunt, and kneeled on the tile floor beside Conner.

CHAPTER FOURTEEN
The Emergency Room Does Not Deal with Squirrels

There was blood everywhere.

Where was it all coming from?

"Conner!"

Marcus grabbed his brother's shoulder, about to shake him. He froze. No, that could make it worse. Marcus scanned his brother for the source. There, a slash above Conner's eyebrow bled into his eyes, dripping on the floor. He had a lump under the cut that was turning purple and swelling up fast.

Conner blinked in groggy confusion then gave a nervous laugh. He rubbed his shirt sleeve across his face, trying to clear the blood. "Guess I look pretty bad."

Marcus breathed a relieved sigh and yanked a clean TP roll out from under the sink. "But you're moving, which is more than we can say for Aunt Stella." He pressed the whole roll to Conner's cut. "Here." His brother held it in place. "Does anything other than your head hurt?"

"Just my thumb. Everything else seems OK."

Aunt Stella sat up and put a hand over her heart. "Oh, my. Let's get you to the doctor, honey."

While Conner attempted to wiggle the sore thumb, Marcus tried to imagine a scenario where his mother wouldn't gasp in horror when she saw his brother's injuries.

Yeah, Mom and Dad were going to be *thrilled*.

Conner did not appear well cared-for, even though he and Aunt Stella had certainly tried. He looked mangled, run over, maimed. Not the calm and content new-puppy owner that their folks were hoping for. More like a fun-loving young version of Frankenstein's Monster.

Phooey Kerflooey

Marcus hefted Phooey out of the van and into his arms, then charged after Aunt Stella as she wheeled Conner into the ER. A nurse stopped him at the spinning door.

"I'm sorry. No dogs." She smiled, but the stern look in her eyes remained firm.

Marcus sighed and lugged Phooey Kerflooey back toward the ER pull-in area where the minivan sat, doors flung open. With a tight grip around her middle, he climbed in and plopped her down on his lap.

What had he been thinking, picking out a puppy?

He stared down at Phooey. She lay curled in his lap, covered in cornmeal and flour, still trembling. He peered through the revolving doors of the ER, where Aunt Stella was standing beside a bruised and bleeding Conner. His face looked really bad. Could his head really be all right after hitting the toilet? And what about his legs and back? Just because he couldn't feel them didn't mean they wouldn't break if he was, say, launched out of his chair while chasing a scaredy pup and rogue squirrel. Marcus didn't want to imagine the possibility of more spinal damage.

Why had Mom trusted him to choose their dog? He'd managed to utterly fail at the job. Just like he'd failed to keep Conner from sneaking out and getting hurt last year.

Choosing their puppy had seemed simple, straightforward. A way to bring peace into their chaos. A way to show his parents that he was a reliable big brother. The breeder had already been paid. Mom had all the research he'd compiled. It should have been easy. He should have been able to walk into a stall full of adorable puppies and take any of them home without causing epic mayhem. A dog was supposed to chase squirrels and love kids no matter what kind of chair they had to sit in. It should have worked.

Instead, he felt like he'd personally brought about the end of the world. Their world, at least. Phooey was the biggest wimp ever, Mom and Dad would be home in a few hours, even Rasputin would die this winter if all he stored up were paintballs.

Maybe not.

That furry tyrant didn't seem like an ordinary squirrel. More like the Squirrel of the Apocalypse.

What if, when the world's final day came, it wasn't four grim horsemen bringing doom, but four giant squirrels? Or even just one squirrel. Huge eyes red with greed, claws scratching, tail flicking in anger.

Rasputin had managed to cause an apocalyptic mess even though he weighed less than a pound. When Mom and Dad got back, they would see end-of-the-world-worthy destruction all across the house with their own eyes if the boys didn't get that rodent caught and everything cleaned up.

Aunt Stella had looked up the cost of a local exterminator and made the unfortunate discovery that he charged 500 to 1,000 dollars for squirrel removal. Marcus knew that after medical bills, buying Mom's special ring that had been put on hold several times due to those bills, and the expense of purchasing Phooey, his parents did not have much left to spend on Rasputin's demise.

That tactic would also mean admitting to Mom that Phooey was useless as a squirrel deterrent. Would Mom put up with too big, too hairy, too slobbery, and too picky if their pup was also too scared to rid them of Rasputin's rampaging?

Marcus gave a grim laugh as he let his forehead thump against the window glass. No, no she would not.

One squirrel was not supposed to cause that much destruction.

Marcus pressed his face into Phooey's gritty fur and wept. He just let the tears and snot and disappointment come full force. When his breathing became something more than choked gasps and his eyes were so puffy he could barely blink, a noise broke into the quiet.

Thump, thump, thump.

Despite her dirty fur and hurting paw, Phooey was wagging.

Her tail thumped against the van door and she nudged her snout up under Marcus's chin, giving him a gentle lick.

Their eyes met.

Phooey whined and hung her head. Then she rolled her eyes up to look at him. She looked so sad. Marcus pulled her close and her tail went into overdrive. "You wanted to be brave, didn't you?"

Phooey lifted her muzzle and gave a low, mournful howl.

"You know what? I thought I'd be a better pet owner, too. What a pair we are, huh?" Phooey snuggled into his chest and Marcus stroked her powdery fur. "Maybe we can be better."

Just then, Aunt Stella heaved open the van door and scrambled for the chairlift remote. "Well, he has a slight concussion, a lot of bruises, four new stitches, and a sprained thumb, but I guess that's a pretty typical week for your brother."

Marcus and Phooey scrambled to the back seat once Conner got settled. Marcus moved Phooey close enough so his brother could scratch her soft ears over the top of the seat. She looked at the chair suspiciously, but stayed for the pets, closing her eyes and leaning into Conner's hand.

Aunt Stella struggled to buckle up, grumbling the whole time. "Those ER doctors know how to clean up a gash and boss you around, but they sure don't have any ideas about squirrels. I asked every medical professional I saw and no one knows who to call to fight off attacking woodland animals. Well, besides that guy who wanted 1,000 dollars and a signed guarantee that Rasputin does not carry bubonic plague. How on earth am I supposed to know if our squirrel is plagued? He certainly is a plague, himself, so you never know. That big, bearded doctor even had the gall to laugh. Some people."

As the van sped home, Marcus clung tight to Phooey and considered their squirrel problem. The invasion had to end. He and Conner and Phooey needed to figure this out. Mom and Dad would be home at nine and all the adults were stumped, including the ER doctors.

So what if he and Conner weren't the best pet owners ever and Phooey wasn't the squirrel-chasing hero they'd expected? They all had a few things to learn, but they could do this.

Phooey hadn't given up on them and they shouldn't give up on her or their quest.

Rasputin had to go. If no one else could do it, they would just have to beat the odds and overcome the Squirrel of the Apocalypse themselves.

CHAPTER FIFTEEN
Squirrel Unleashed

When Aunt Stella unlocked the front door, Rasputin scampered across the entryway with a whole bagel clamped in his jaws.

Marcus clutched Phooey tighter. The entryway? How had the squirrel gotten to the entryway unless he'd crossed . . . Mom's showroom! Had they left the sliding door ajar?

Marcus stumbled inside. Something crunched under his feet.

He slammed his eyes shut. There was absolutely nothing in this room that should crunch. He looked down.

No patch of flooring, whether carpeted or linoleum, was free of some gritty substance. Cornmeal, brown sugar, twisty noodles, sports drink mix, and baking soda were just a few of the ingredients he spotted. How? Surely Rasputin didn't eat baking soda!

Aunt Stella wobbled to a stop, leaving Conner's chair halfway on the doorstep with one front wheel spinning slowly in the air. Conner whispered, apparently struck quiet by the sheer destruction, "Thy sin's not accidental, but a trade. Would thou wert clean enough to spit upon."

Marcus bent to let Phooey slide from his arms into an indignant heap at his feet. He closed his eyes, willing the destruction away. But when he pulled Phooey back into his arms and opened them once more, he could not deny the truth.

Rasputin had not left Mom's perfect lavender and gray showroom unscathed.

Absolutely everything was thoroughly scathed.

The destruction was beyond what he imagined an entire army of squirrels could accomplish. The pale gray carpet was bright with a dusting of crumbly things. On the couch, a box of chewed noodles spilled across the cushions and several pieces of dried fruit stuck to the fabric in unsavory globs. Chew marks marred the coffee table's glossy eagle feet and one of the moth paintings had crashed to the floor. Marcus peered closer. Rasputin had nibbled the leaves off the pressed flowers and chewed a huge hole right through one of the painted moths.

Aunt Stella gave a strangled cry as she hobbled into the kitchen and beheld the state of the pantry. Her hands shook when she crouched to retrieve a mangled bag of croutons and a small plastic shaker of basil that leaked green flakes from the chewed-up top. She glanced up at the clock and then sagged against the counter. She still had smears of blood from Conner's injury on her shirt. A little had even dried in her hair. Aunt Stella rested her forehead against the fridge for a moment, a look of pure exhaustion covering her face. "That squirrel left us nothing to eat, unless you boys want that jar of pepperoncinis from the fridge."

Marcus and Conner looked at each other. Was that a real question? Should they answer? More importantly, should they answer honestly? But instead of interrogating them further about the pickled pepper option, their aunt marched to the counter, brushed some squirrel poo off the phone book, and found a number Mom had written in permanent ink on the inside cover.

"It's getting late, boys. We'll just have to order pizza." She ran her fingers back through her hair but they stuck. "Give me a moment to wash the blood out of my hair and then we can get some food inside us. You boys see if there's any place remotely clean that we can set the food when it comes." With a groan, Aunt Stella trundled off toward the guestroom shower.

A few minutes later, Marcus was setting up five-gallon buckets around a card table in the laundry room when he heard Aunt Stella start whistling in the shower. She must have left the bedroom door cracked just enough for the sound to escape. At least she seemed to be feeling better.

Phooey cocked her head to the side and stood, still as a statue.

"Do you like music, girl?" Marcus asked.

Phooey lowered her head and peered down the hall toward the guestroom, her tail straight out behind her.

Aunt Stella began a whistled version of *Ride of the Valkyries*.

Phooey tensed up, her body trembling. She crouched, flattened her ears, and then launched past the boys and around the corner.

Marcus met Conner's startled gaze. "That was weird! Do you think we should check on Aunt Stella?"

"What could happen? It's not like we could check on her in the shower, right?" Conner shrugged.

"That's true. Phooey must just love her whistling. You know, if Phooey had her princess music, we might get some sleep tonight." Marcus glanced at his brother, hoping for a hint about the location of the hidden CDs and doll baby. Mom could make a princess movie playlist on her phone, but would she after seeing the additional chaos their pup had brought? "As it is, you might have to park by her crate and whistle all night." Nothing. Conner didn't give away a thing.

Marcus set three plates and three glasses on the card table. He was about to head to the kitchen for the silverware when an alarming noise filled the house. Half avalanche and half scuffing plastic.

He peeked into the hall. A large green-and-yellow tent thundered straight toward him. Were those . . . rubber duckies on the tent fabric? The galloping mass shot past. A new noise filled the silence. Someone was choking! The gasps morphed into a long, drawn-out scream.

Marcus ran toward the guestroom, Conner wheeling right behind.

"No," Aunt Stella shouted. "Don't come in here, boys. Gracious gophers! I'm not decent."

They screeched to a halt. How could they help without venturing inside?

"Just chase down that mutt and get back my shower curtain!"

The shower curtain. Now the yellow duckies made sense.

Marcus and Conner did an about-face and rushed back the way they'd come. The Phooey-tent-shower curtain combo had been headed toward the bedrooms.

Mom and Dad's room had been ransacked. Squirrel poos, torn tissue, and a growing pile of paintballs lay scattered around the floor, but no shower curtain.

Marcus paused a moment, considering grabbing another TP doll for Phooey. But no, it would get chewed up and they belonged to Aunt Stella.

Finally, the boys discovered a rumpled heap on Conner's bed. It was breathing. Marcus peeked underneath the plastic. Phooey's eyes were huge. She trembled and gave him the tiniest little whine before hiding her nose under her big front paws.

Marcus pulled her out of the tangled curtain while Conner wadded it up and set it in his lap. "I'll just go and, you know, stuff it through the door for Aunt Stella."

"Just a sec." Marcus darted out of the room and grabbed a sleeping mask off Mom's nightstand. "Here, wear this."

Conner snapped the mask over his eyes and rolled to the guestroom.

Marcus gathered a shivering Phooey into his arms. "What are we going to do with you, girl? Aunt

Stella is your biggest ally. You shouldn't have scared her."

Phooey gave him a big slurp across the face as he hauled her toward the laundry room. Halfway there, she got spooked by a scratching noise behind the wall, escaped his arms, and thundered away. He watched her drooping tail disappear around the corner. He'd find her in a minute. He had to finish getting the laundry room ready for dinner. Marcus was so hungry and so tired of that squirrel. A few moments to eat in peace—that was all he wanted. Just the tiniest glimpse of calm.

As he entered the kitchen to grab the silverware, the phone rang. Aunt Stella stumbled out of the guestroom to answer it, wrapped in a bright orange bathrobe, her hair dripping. She got louder and louder as the call went on. Marcus could hear her all the way from the laundry room as he finished setting the table. "Of course I gave you the correct address. 364 Larch Lane. No, no, no. That is Larch Street, and watch out for Larch Avenue if you're headed toward the park. Now, if you'll just take a right by the library. Yes, the public library. No, that one belongs to a private school. Are you even in the right town, dear?"

A moment later, the laundry room door flew open and Aunt Stella leaned in. "Oh, it looks wonderful in here. I can't wait to use that little table." Her smile became a glower and her hair continued to drip, making a wet patch on the neck of her blouse. "I have to meet Lisa, the pizza girl, at the park. She's having a bit of trouble finding us and I'm starved. I bet you two are near collapse. I know young boys get so hungry."

Marcus knew it, too. His stomach had started growling an hour ago. He was about ready to attack those pepperoncinis Aunt Stella had offered.

"Don't chase that squirrel while I'm gone! We don't need more bloodshed and mayhem. I'll be right back." She breezed out.

With Aunt Stella gone, they would have to be extra cautious. Marcus pulled his notebook out of his back pocket and snatched the pencil from under his shoelaces. He wrote: *Dangers of Battling a Squirrel: 1) Nowhere clean to sit, 2) No food, 3) General destruction, 4) Sprains, 5) Bruises, 6) Stitches, 7) Concussion.* Yep, all those things had already happened. Marcus swallowed hard and put his notebook and pencil away.

Perhaps he should just put Phooey on a leash. And maybe Conner, too. If only the squirrel hadn't dragged all the popcorn kernels out and dumped them into the cushions of Mom's overstuffed chair. He could have bribed them both with a snack and cartoons.

Shutting the laundry room door so Rasputin wouldn't mess up their dinner spot, Marcus went to find his brother and Phooey.

He found Phooey in the showroom, cowering under the coffee table, and Conner trying to coax her near his wheelchair with a rubber ball tied to a string.

The doorbell rang. The one on the front door. The door that opened into Mom's ransacked showroom.

Marcus peeked his head out of the hall and stared at the door. He shouldn't answer it when Aunt Stella was gone. But what if it was the pizza girl, or an emergency? He went to a side window and peeked out. Nia stood on the doorstep. She had a pink gift bag under one arm and her ball and glove in the other.

Well, Nia wasn't exactly a burglar, and it was starting to rain. Marcus opened the door.

It wasn't just Nia.

A silver-haired lady stood beside Nia. She looked very fancy in a pale yellow suit, with pearls around her neck and a feathered hat perched on her head.

"Hey, Marcus. This is Grandma Florence and she's just dying to see your mom's . . . " Nia's voice trailed off as she glanced over Marcus's shoulder. Her eyes blinked and her mouth formed a small *O*.

Grandma Florence raised an eyebrow at Marcus's bedraggled state and gripped the doorframe with one bejeweled hand. "Is your mother here, young man?"

Nia sprang into action, literally. She twirled, making the tutu she wore over her jeans bounce, then leaped off the front stoop. "Grandma Florence, look!" she said before immediately going into a tap dance routine across the decorative rocks in their yard.

Marcus stood tall, thankful for Nia's quick thinking. Those rocks were a terrible surface to dance on and Nia hadn't had tap lessons. She must be making it all up. Yep, Nia added three cartwheels and some jumping jacks to her routine.

Marcus faced Grandma Florence. "No, ma'am. But she should be back soon. I mean, not too soon, but sort of soon." He blinked up at her, trying to come up with the amazing magical words that would fix the horrendous situation and transform his mom's living room back into the impressive showpiece it had been a few hours before.

"Are you quite alright? You're not alone, are you?" Grandma Florence took a step forward. Crunch. She looked down and gave a small gasp clutching at her pearls. "Well, I'll just come back later then." She straightened her hat, turned away, and glided across the street, her heels clacking against the pavement. They seemed to ring out the end of Mom's chances at designing anything for Nia's family.

Clack, clack, clack . . . No, no, no.

Marcus pressed his forehead against the doorframe and groaned.

"Hey," Nia said. She'd stopped dancing and had a concerned look on her face. "I brought something for Phooey."

Marcus slowly looked up. Oh, wow. Nia was still standing right in front of him, holding up the bag.

"Are you guys all right?" She scowled, glancing first at Marcus's face and then the flour and cornmeal that coated his shoes.

"We're awesome." Why had he said that? Awesome at destroying a perfectly good house, maybe. "Awesome" didn't really describe anything other than the giant mess inside. He blocked the door and tried to smile. He probably looked less like a responsible young puppy owner and more like an angry circus clown whose face paint had been applied by baboons. OK, so smiling was out. How could he make her go away before she realized just how thoroughly they'd failed at both puppy training and squirrel capture?

"So . . . if you guys are awesome, then why is that squirrel running back and forth behind you with a bag of croutons?"

Marcus spun. A fluffy tail disappeared under the couch and Phooey whined and quaked in terror beneath the coffee table.

"Perhaps awesome isn't the exact word I was looking for. How about we're 'catastrophic failures.' Does that have a better ring to it?"

"Are you gonna let me in or just keep on ignoring that squirrel?" Nia squinted over his shoulder, "and the full-sized bag of crinkle-cut potato chips that it's lugging past your dog?"

Phooey curled into a little ball, moaning and trembling. She even flopped her tail across her nose so it hid her eyes. "She's really scared of the squirrel, isn't she?" Nia said.

"Yeah, and Conner's wheelchair and the linoleum and any TV show that has explosions or dancing or green peppers. But she does like giant jawbreakers." Marcus looked at Nia for a moment and then sighed. "Come on in." He held the door open so she could view the full extent of the destruction Rasputin and Phooey had wrought.

"Oh, wow." Nia crossed the entryway and tried to navigate through the scattered snack items until she reached the couch. She bent down to look under the coffee table where Phooey cowered.

The squirrel darted past with an entire roll of toilet paper in its jaws.

"Why don't you get one of her special things the breeder sent?"

"Oh, well . . . They broke." Which was not a complete lie, he supposed. He had heard something snap when he was stuffing the doll in the trash. "She was getting so brave, I didn't think she needed all that stuff." His chest felt suddenly tight. That was definitely a lie. Instead of further falsehoods, he pointed at Phooey hopefully.

Nia assessed the trembling puppy with a critical eye. "She did peer out from under her tail for a moment. Maybe she's finding her courage. I think she has an eye on that old Cheerio the squirrel just dropped."

Nia and Marcus sat on the couch and watched, hardly breathing, awaiting Phooey's brave battle for the piece of breakfast cereal.

Phooey flattened herself and inched her paws out from under the coffee table. Then came her big black nose, sniffing loudly as it zeroed in on the tasty tidbit. Closer and closer, Phooey advanced. Her thick tail began to wag, even though her bottom was still under the coffee table. Only a few more inches! Maybe she was growing into the brave dog they needed.

A shrill chittering cry sounded from the hallway. Phooey froze.

The squirrel charged into the room, whipping its fluffy tail around and gnashing its little teeth.

Phooey spronged straight into the air, trying to turn around, run, and fly all at the same time.

Rasputin didn't pause to consider that Phooey outweighed him by twenty-one pounds and four ounces. He attacked. The squirrel sprang to the top of Phooey's furry head and started savaging one of her ears with his vicious little claws and biting at her snout.

Phooey made a sound of pure terror. Not quite a bark or a howl or a whine. More like a mix between a broken lawnmower, a pack of wolves being overrun by rampaging bison, and a lost kitten in the carwash.

Marcus lunged forward to help, but Phooey was too fast.

Their new pup fled for her life. Around and around the coffee table, across Nia's lap, right up

Marcus's chest and over his head, then into the wood bin where she burrowed underneath a bunch of kindling and old newspapers.

Nia gave him a knowing look. "She needs her doll baby. Wherever you hid it, dig it out."

"Conner took the TP doll, OK? I gave it to her and Conner hid it. I don't have any idea where it's at." Marcus lowered his head into his hands and sighed. He hadn't meant to tell Nia. Hadn't meant to badmouth his brother or leave his dog doll-less or fail everyone. Why was this all so impossible? He couldn't make everyone happy, or anyone happy, no matter what he did. "Phooey was supposed to make everything so calm and peaceful, but it's been a chaos hurricane since we brought her home. I never should have picked her."

"Phooey's a good dog, just not a perfect dog. You can't make everything perfect, Marcus." Nia gave a sad smile. "She's not a peace machine, just an amazing creature God made. Don't lose a wonderful pet 'cause you're waiting for her to be something she's not."

Marcus glanced at the wood box. It was rattling with all of Phooey's fearful trembling. "Gee, thanks, Nia." Now that she'd pointed out how imperfect everything was, would Nia finally leave?

She sighed and handed over the small baggy.

"I found some more bows for her in my closet. Clip them right above her ear. She'll look adorable." Nia paused for a moment, staring at the pile of kindling where Phooey had hidden herself. "Now, don't laugh at me." She glanced at Marcus and glared.

He nodded, promising not to laugh.

"Well, there was something in the Sunday School lesson that reminds me of Phooey."

Marcus blinked. That seemed unlikely, but he carefully kept himself from laughing. Despite the oddness of her statement, he wasn't sure he'd feel like laughing, anyway, no matter how many strange things she said.

"The teacher was talking about how the church is made up of a whole bunch of different people, just like a body is made up of lots of different parts. The verse said not to be jealous of the eye or the hand, if God made you to be a foot. What if you can't change her? What if she isn't the chomping teeth of the body? Maybe she's the waggy tail."

"She has to be the chomping teeth, Nia. Conner needs her to be the chomping teeth and I need Conner to slow down for just a minute. Is that too much? Just a moment of peace. He likes dogs. I like dogs. Phooey is our only hope."

"Yeah, but what if you can't change Conner, either?"

Marcus looked away. "I don't know what you're talking about."

"I tried to change him, too, you know."

Marcus looked back. He remembered. Nia had bedazzled Conner's shoes and Conner had painted her pink backpack the ugliest olive green. The madness had continued nonstop before it culminated in a tragic sparkle-paint incident that pushed their parents over the edge. Nia and Conner weren't allowed to play together for a month. They'd stopped after that, their friendship intact despite Nia's sparkles and Conner's shouted Shakespeare.

"What if God's peace is in the middle of everything?" Nia said. "What if God's peace isn't the calm kind?"

Marcus stared at their neighbor, a catch in his throat. He knew the verse she was talking about. But that didn't mean that Conner would be happy with the "waggy tail of the body" instead of the "chomping teeth." Despite his efforts to forget it, Nia's verse marched across his mind.

If the whole body were an eye, how would you hear? Or if your whole body were an ear, how would you smell anything? But our bodies have many parts, and God has put each part just where he wants it.

"You guys want some help cleaning up?" she asked.

Marcus shook his head automatically. "Nope, we're great."

No! That wasn't true at all. They totally needed help. Maybe Nia would ask again if he waited.

"Well, I'll check on you guys later," Nia said. "Call if you need anything and, um . . . have fun. I'm just going to go and see how Grandma Florence is doing." Nia glanced around the living room before carefully tiptoeing through the rubble and out the front door.

Marcus walked over to the wood box and scooped Phooey out. He should have asked for help. What was wrong with him? And now what should he do?

Phooey was a wonderful dog, just not an overly brave one. He sat down on Mom's couch with the big pup in his lap. She loved to gallop around Conner's bed and hide her dog bone under his pillow. Phooey was adorable when she pranced across the floor with the TP doll. But Mom had wanted her to chase away the squirrel and help Conner. Phooey was supposed to guard their house and make his little brother calm. Dolls did not make Conner calm.

Something squeezed inside Marcus's chest, aching and tight. He loved Phooey exactly the way she was. He thought about how her eyes lit up when she spotted one of them eating a baby carrot, how her tail wagged whenever they praised her for almost sitting or almost staying or almost lying down, and how she slurped their ears whenever they bent close. Were other puppies able to communicate an entire sentence, "More belly rubs, please?" with a single raised eyebrow? Marcus didn't think so. Phooey was special.

But funny, furry, and sweet hadn't made Conner's list as he'd described the perfect puppy while they'd crowded around the pile of dog-training books last week. Strong, fierce, bold, stern, athletic, and capable of overthrowing a small army of woodland creatures and ruling them with an iron paw *had* been on the list. Adorable wasn't what his brother wanted.

Marcus had to help Phooey be brave. Brave enough to fight Rasputin for Mom and brave enough to help Conner face life in his chair without always needing to wheel into danger every moment of every day. Marcus thought about pulling out his notebook and pencil to write down the hazards of such a project. He looked into Phooey's big brown eyes. No.

After everything Conner had been through, after Marcus had slept right through the one time Conner had needed him the most, didn't his brother deserve this? No matter how he felt about her, Marcus had to train Phooey into the pup his brother needed. That meant sacrifices—from both of them.

"I would get you the doll baby," he whispered. "I really would. I think it's cute. But then I'd be letting you revert into complete wimpiness."

Phooey slurped his face. Then the squirrel bounded across the floor with a fridge magnet in its jaws. She cringed and burrowed until her head was buried in Marcus's armpit.

"Then again, I don't know that you would be reverting into wimpiness at all. It seems like that is pretty much your natural state, huh, girl?" Phooey wagged her tail and gave his side a sniffle and a tickly snort.

CHAPTER SIXTEEN
Phooey Smells Danger

Marcus tried to pull Phooey out of his armpit. Her nervous snorting tickled.

Unfortunately, the squirrel gave an aggressive trill and Phooey just buried herself deeper. She scrambled with her front paws, rooting at his side with her nose and shoving against his legs with her back paws.

Marcus collapsed onto the couch, laughing. He wrestled the panicking pup onto his lap and covered her in a velvety blanket. "There, girl, you're safe now."

Phooey Kerflooey

The blanket moved like a clock pendulum as her broad tail wagged underneath it. Marcus lifted one corner and looked into Phooey's deep brown eyes.

"Maybe we can still make everyone happy," he told the big furball.

Everyone except Phooey, part of him said.

No, Phooey was young, she had time grow and change. With hard work, she would learn to obey and potty outside and not run from scary flooring and squirrels. "If you help catch the squirrel, maybe you'll realize that you can be brave, too." Then everyone really would be happy. Mom and Conner and even Phooey.

Marcus turned Phooey around so that her head poked out, instead of digging into his armpit. "There you go, girl. I bet you feel braver already."

Phooey swept her tail back and forth and then flinched as the squirrel poked his twitchy little nose around the corner.

"See him? This time, I want *you* to do the chasing." He set Phooey down on the floor and got on his hands and knees beside her. "Like this." Marcus lowered his head and growled, then galloped across the carpet on his hands and knees, straight at the squirrel.

The squirrel was not amused. He chittered and shook his tail, an angry gleam in his eye. Right as Marcus plunged around the corner, his imaginary dog teeth snapping, the squirrel attacked.

Rasputin darted up Marcus's arm, scratched around in his hair, and clamped little squirrely teeth onto his ear.

Marcus yelled and swatted at the aggressive rodent.

His attacker jumped off his head and departed with an arrogant flip of his tail.

Marcus flopped over on his back, panting. Great, hadn't the ER doctor said squirrels carried bubonic plague? He'd have to be on high alert for any flu-like symptoms!

A huge, furry shadow loomed over him. It lowered its head tentatively. Looked left and then right and then left again. Then Phooey flopped onto his chest, slurping his face and neck and wounded ear.

"Well, I'm sure it will go much better for you, Phooey, since you're an actual dog." He heaved himself up with a groan and pointed her in the right direction. After a long pause, Marcus gave her furry rump a little shove.

Phooey got going, all right. She spotted the squirrel, did a kind of flip-turn midair, and galloped in the opposite direction. She then hid under the coffee table and had an accident.

Marcus stared at the huge puddle, his heart hammering in his ears. Mom's carpet! Her perfect carpet in her perfect room! She was always talking about how carpeting was never really the same once it had encountered something sticky or stinky.

He glanced at the floor again, taking in the blue powdered sports drink mix, Italian bread crumbs, and deep-fried Chinese noodles. "I'll just, you know, get the paper towels."

The puddle was easy to see, since it was spreading across the carpet, but Phooey was remarkably well-hidden for such a large animal. Twenty-two pounds of frightened fluff. A big black nose, that was all he could really see of Phooey in her hiding spot.

After sopping up the puddle and spraying the area with white vinegar, Marcus resumed their squirrel-chasing lesson while Conner took a quick nap to recover from his recent head injury.

Marcus located Rasputin in the bathroom. The hairy tyrant was darting in and out of Mom's fancy bath powder, coating his tail in white, making a lilac-scented cloud that hovered over the whole room, and getting squirrel poos in the powder puff.

"Are you gonna let him get away with that?" Marcus asked, sitting down on the floor and positioning Phooey in front of him.

Phooey yelped and burrowed under his shirt.

"You have to overcome your fear and you have to do it now," Marcus whispered as he tried to pry the fat puppy out from under his shirt. "Mom and Dad are coming home tonight." He put Phooey down and blocked the door so she couldn't run. "Get him, girl. You can do it. We've got to catch that squirrel." He scooted Phooey toward the squirrel. She gave a tentative bark and then flattened herself against the floor.

The squirrel rose up out of the powder like a horrible, chattering ghost. Rasputin paused dramatically and then bounced toward them, flipping his tail.

Marcus felt something wet soak his foot. "No, no, no. This is not how it's supposed to go." He looked down. A huge, stinky puddle spread across the floor underneath Phooey.

When he was distracted by the mess, she made a break for it. Galloping off down the hallway leaving powdery pee footprints all the way to the coffee table.

Marcus stomped after her, cleaning supplies in hand.

The house phone rang, but he ignored it. He couldn't talk to anyone right now, not when everything was so completely messed up that he didn't have an answer to the simplest questions. Questions like, "Are you OK?" and "How are things going?"

After cleaning up the mess and rinsing Phooey's paws, belly, and urine-soaked tail in the sink, Marcus sagged onto the floor and let his head sink into his hands.

Phooey Kerflooey

The phone rang again.

What was he doing? This was never going to work. Phooey simply did not have what it took. Rasputin was going to ruin their house and there was nothing anyone, especially Phooey, could do about it.

Their ancient answering machine kicked in and took the call, right as Conner wheeled around the corner. Mom's voice sounded tired as she left a message.

"So, boys. Aunt Stella just texted me. I also got several calls from Nia's grandmother. I'm so sorry that you were hurt, Conner, but so incredibly glad you're going to be all right. I hear there was a mix-up with the puppies. Now, don't get attached, boys. I know this puppy isn't what you wanted. It sounds like she's too big and hairy and slobbery and not very brave. That won't do at all. There is a Scottie breeder right here in town. I just got off the phone with them and they told me that fearlessness is a characteristic of the breed. I can't believe I thought Newfoundlands and Scotties were the same dog. I did love the Newfie breeder's description of sweet mountains of love, I just didn't realize that she literally meant the dog was a mountain. OK, boys. I'll see you at bedtime and we'll take the puppy back tomorrow. The Newfoundland breeder says there is a family with four kids who would love to have her. Then we can go get that Scottie."

The answering machine gave a long beep, then silence held the room.

Outside, the wind picked up and sheets of rain slashed against the windows.

Marcus and Conner looked at each other, then at the coffee table where Phooey was hiding.

Her tail and one hind paw stuck out.

Marcus swallowed hard. There was a solution. They didn't have to keep trying to turn Phooey into a fierce squirrel-hunter. Mom could simply take her back. Phooey would go home with another family and he and Conner would get a fierce Scottish terrier. A happy ending for everyone.

Marcus's throat tightened as he glanced up at Conner. He blinked some moisture away and attempted a smile.

His brother looked strangely pale.

Phooey Kerflooey

Phooey's furry tail thumped from under the coffee table and Marcus leaned over and pulled her out.

"Would you like that, girl?" he asked, patting her soft head. "You could have a whole passel of kids all to yourself." Phooey scrambled up his chest and slurped his face. Then she plopped into his lap with a sigh, curled in a furry ball, and fell fast asleep.

Rasputin skittered around the corner.

Phooey woke with a start and cringed. Then she paused. She peered out from under Marcus's armpit, inched farther and farther, then she froze with her nose pointing at the squirrel. Phooey let loose three fierce barks and then scooted inside his shirt, trembling.

"Good girl." Marcus gave her a pat. "You almost had him there." He sighed. She was doing her best. Phooey just wasn't a guard dog. Maybe they should just say goodbye.

The squirrel dragged something past them down the hall. Marcus squinted. Was that a wire? Where would the squirrel get a wire, and why? They weren't edible. It wasn't like the creature was going to build something or run power to his nest or anything.

The lights flickered.

Marcus could hear the trees in Nia's yard thrashing back and forth in the stormy weather.

Phooey shivered and curled into an even tighter ball.

"It's OK, girl. Probably just the wind." He stroked Phooey's head and pulled her close.

There was a quiet crackling noise from somewhere in the house. The lights flickered again and a strange smell drifted down the hall. It burned his nose and made him think of failed cooking experiments and outdoor camping trips.

Phooey sniffed loudly and then began to whine.

"Stop squeezing her," Conner said.

"I'm not. I was just patting her head. Between the two of us, who is more likely to squeeze her too hard?"

Conner glared at him and Marcus tried to keep Phooey calm while returning the look.

There was another crackle. The lights stuttered and blinked. With a loud pop, half the house went completely dark.

Phooey gave a sniff and followed it up with a long howl.

A sound like a tree crashing to the ground came from just outside. Nia's tree? Oh, no!

The rest of the house went dark.

Marcus tried to keep her still but Phooey wiggled free and ran into the darkness, sniffing all the while.

"Phooey, come. Come now!" He charged in the direction he thought she'd gone but skidded to a stop. What was that smell? It couldn't be smoke. Why would there be smoke in the house? No one was making toast and there wasn't a fire in the fireplace. Marcus heard an angry chitter.

The squirrel.

The wire.

It was smoke!

He shouted for his brother and hit the floor, crawling on his hands and knees, searching for Phooey in the smoke-tinged darkness.

CHAPTER SEVENTEEN
Phooey Goes Kerflooey

Marcus crawled back toward the living room, shouting for his brother.

"I'm right here," Conner said behind him, making Marcus jump and whack his head on an end table near one of the overstuffed chairs. Conner coughed. "Is that smoke?"

"Yeah, and Phooey just ran off. We've got to catch her, call 911, and get out of the house."

"If there's a fire, we should put it out. We can't let that rampallian win." Conner's tone was cold with anger.

"Only if it's safe. We find Phooey and check out that smoke. If we're in danger we call 911 and leave, all right?"

An empty quiet that filled the dark room was his brother's only answer. So much for negotiating and reason.

The silence grew heavy. Marcus froze, listening. He heard a scratching from the living room. The squirrel or Phooey? Then a whimper. "She's here somewhere. Probably under the coffee table."

"You grab her. I'll see about that smoke."

"No, we've got to stick together. You can't just—" Marcus heard wheelchair tires zipping away. Great. He crawled double-time, feeling the carpet in front of him for their hiding pup. If he got her quickly, he could go help Conner. His fingers brushed fur, then his cheekbone smashed into a hard edge. Ouch! That would be the coffee table.

Marcus groped underneath and grabbed a paw. He patted around until he found Phooey's chubby middle, then grabbed her tight. There, one lost pup found. Now to secure her and get Conner.

Marcus shuffled down the hall, lugging Phooey. He walked with one shoulder against the wall and groped forward with his feet so that he wouldn't smack into anything in the dark. Where was her leash? He paused, thinking back over the day. He'd forgotten to take it to the ER . . . It must still be hanging on their bunk.

He rushed forward and stumbled as the wall he'd been leaning against disappeared. A doorway. Phooey whined and twisted in his arms. Marcus was halfway into the room before he caught his balance and hefted Phooey up against his shoulder. His arm brushed against a cold, hard surface. The bathroom sink. Phooey was really fighting now, squirming and thrashing, trying to get under the sink.

Marcus hauled her to their room and found the leash. He felt for the loop on her collar and clipped the leash in place. There, now she couldn't run away again.

Where was Conner? Marcus heard some muttered Shakespear, and he hurried forward, keeping one hand on the wall for guidance and the other gripping Phooey's leash.

He rounded the corner and froze. An odd, flickering light illuminated the kitchen and part of the hallway. He could see Conner just ahead, barreling down the hall toward the eerie glow.

"Conner, get back!" Marcus charged forward and grabbed his brother's arm.

Conner fought. "We've got to find the fire. The whole house could burn!"

"And us with it. We should call 911 then get outside."

"There's barely any smoke. We can put it out."

Marcus pulled back on his brother's chair and Conner strained to wheel forward. Phooey kept tangling her leash around his feet and Conner's chair.

They jerked back and forth just outside the kitchen, lurching forward an inch, then sliding back two. Conner reached back and thumped Marcus with one of Phooey's squeaky toys. Marcus let go for an instant and Conner sped forward shouting out brave bits of Shakespeare into the darkness. "Cry 'Havoc!', and let slip the dogs of war!"

Phooey galumphed beside Marcus as he darted after Conner. Conner's ridiculous battle cry had his mind spinning and his heart thumping wildly. They didn't even have any dogs of war to "let slip." Phooey wasn't exactly a war dog, and she'd better not slip her collar. Unless it was a metaphor. Ugh! None of that mattered. They had to get out of here.

Marcus lunged and snagged a wheelchair handle, almost tripping over Phooey.

Conner's chair tipped, teetering on edge.

Marcus's breath caught in his throat as he let go to allow the wheelchair to right itself.

That was all it took for Conner to be off again.

Marcus shoved past Conner and blocked the doorway to the kitchen. He was ready to immobilize his brother's chair in a flying tackle when something gave him pause.

You can't make everything perfect, Marcus.

He froze and slowly slid his glasses back onto the bridge of his nose with a finger. Was Nia right?

With his heart pounding hard and adrenaline rushing through his veins, everything else seemed to slow down while his mind went into overdrive.

If the whole body were an eye, where would the hearing be? If the whole were hearing, where would the sense of smell be? But now God has placed the members, each one of them, in the body, just as He desired.

He had wondered how David found peace when he stood to face Goliath.

David had chosen to be exactly who God made him: a shepherd boy with a sling. He hadn't worn King Saul's fancy armor and hadn't taken the sword they'd offered. David had simply stood between a giant and the army of Israel—and trusted God.

Marcus thought of Mom's shiny wooden plaque about peace. In his quest for calm and quiet, he'd forgotten to consider the ending.

You will keep in perfect peace . . . all whose thoughts are fixed on you. —Isaiah 26:3

Thoughts fixed on God. Just like David while the giant scoffed. A shepherd boy simply being a shepherd boy, but one focused totally on God.

Perhaps God had plans for them, too. Could His peace survive the accident-prone antics, embarrassing toilet-paper doll, lack of squirrel-catching skills, and everything? And that night, a year ago, when Marcus had slept through his brother's escape and been buried under the weight of it? Maybe even that hadn't changed God's plans for him.

Dad's words from when they found out Conner would need a wheelchair came rushing back. He'd heard them last spring. But now, with the flickering light illuminating his little brother's angry face and the smell of smoke drifting through the quiet house, Marcus finally understood.

Maybe if we'd all been perfect, we could have stopped him, Dad had said. *You didn't wake up. I agree. But you were supposed to be sleeping. That was your only job that night—to sleep. I was awake. Maybe if I hadn't been listening to a podcast on Himalayan Yeti myths, I would have heard him. I didn't. Do you still want me for your dad? You and Conner aren't perfect, but I wouldn't trade you boys for anything. Can you trust God with this, even though He gave you to a family that's not perfect?*

Had Marcus been so focused on perfect peace that he'd not only tried to make Phooey into something she wasn't, but Conner, as well? Maybe brothers didn't just stick together. Maybe brothers trusted each other, too.

Marcus shut his eyes against the wavering glow behind him and the smoke in the air. *What do you want, God? What do you want from me right now?* A quiet. A steadiness. A certainty settled around him. Marcus opened his eyes and faced his brother.

"Fine," Marcus said, "but we call 911 and we go in together. At the first sign this is too much to handle, we take Phooey outside. She's just a puppy and needs our help."

Conner blew his breath out and then nodded in agreement.

Slowly, the two brothers and their trembling pup faced the glow in the darkness. They advanced together into the kitchen. The smell of smoke grew thicker and the room was filled with yellow light and flickering shadows. Where was it coming from? The power was off, wasn't it?

Hanging off the counter, where Aunt Stella had been mixing up pancake batter before she realized Rasputin had ruined the new bag of flour, was a hand mixer. The mixer swung from the wall socket, and the bowl and ingredients were scattered. But the mess wasn't what made Marcus's heart lurch in his chest.

The mixer's cord showed exposed wires as if something had chewed it open. It must have been sparking before the power went off.

A nearby trash can emitted the flickering glow. As Marcus tried to acknowledge what he was seeing, Conner barreled past him. His brother pulled off his sweatshirt and dunked it in the sink. "Turn on the faucet. We've got to get this out."

Marcus dragged Phooey to the sink and pulled the tap. Water soaked the sweatshirt and Conner wheeled toward the burning garbage can.

Marcus clicked on the camping lantern Dad kept in the far corner of the counter. In the brighter light, he found their old cordless phone. Mom and Dad had cells, but this was the one the boys used. Marcus grabbed the phone off its base and held it to his ear. Nothing. It was dead. No power, no cordless phone. And Aunt Stella had taken her cell.

Heart thudding way too fast, Marcus snatched a kitchen towel and drenched it, as well. Both boys beat at the flames as they rose out of the can, licking higher and higher.

On the end of her leash, Phooey thrashed. She did not approve of the plan. Something in the garbage can sizzled and then gave a loud pop.

Phooey bolted, yanking the leash off of Marcus's wrist.

"Phooey, no!" Conner wheeled after their pup, leaving the crackling fire behind.

Marcus stared at the dancing flames, maybe if he just kept grabbing soggy towels and threw them into the garbage can one after the other. He inched toward the flaming trash can, dripping towel in hand.

Phooey yipped.

"It's OK girl," Conner said. "Here, let me just—" A loud crash followed. Then Phooey made a horrible crying sound like she was dying via bear attack.

Marcus dropped the towel, grabbed the lantern, and was running before his brain had a chance to realize what his legs had done. Visions of Conner hurt and broken filled his mind. He shoved his glasses back in place and tried to blink away the image of Phooey, bleeding and scared and needing her boys.

Sounds of frantic clawing, terrified growls, and angry chittering came from the bathroom. Was the squirrel attacking Phooey? A sad yip preceded a thump. Then a groan and a long, loud *crack*, as though something solid had bent and snapped.

That disturbing sound was followed by gurgling.

Marcus tore toward the bathroom. What had that evil squirrel done now?

CHAPTER EIGHTEEN
Phooey's Fearsome "Sit" of Destruction

The sound of rushing water filled the hall.

Actual rushing water followed the sound.

Marcus's shoes squeaked as he ran through what felt like a squishy stretch of moss rather than a tastefully decorated home. His feet were soaked in an instant. Splashing noises blended with howls and aggressive chittering.

Marcus stopped at the bathroom doorway. He swept his light through the darkness.

Phooey was digging and thrashing underneath the sink.

Conner leaned way out of his chair trying to grab her.

Marcus leaped to help. "Why's she under the sink?" He reached past a forceful spray of icy water that gushed from a broken pipe.

"I hid her TP doll there!" Conner shouted over the sound of gurgling water, panicking puppy, and angry squirrel.

If Phooey got hurt because Conner hid that silly doll . . . Marcus hit his knees and reached for their soggy dog. She darted away, past Marcus, past Conner, yipping and jumping and scared.

In her bid for her dolly, their pup had tangled her leash around the pipe and broken it free. The cracked pipe bounced around behind her as she sloshed in frantic circles, the evil squirrel nipping at her tail.

A waterfall gushed from under the sink. It pooled on the bathroom floor like a small lake and then surged down the hallway in an unlikely flash flood.

Phooey galumphed onto a rumpled towel and turned to face her attacker, huge paws wide, head lowered, tail drooping behind her.

Rasputin braced himself on top of the toilet seat. Tiny brown paws firm, rodent teeth bared. He bounced forward, his tail snapping with every high, angry trill.

Phooey hung her head and then glanced up, her eyes big and sad. Marcus splashed forward and unclipped the leash from Phooey's collar, freeing her from the broken pipe.

A rubber ducky sailed past Marcus's ear from behind. Then a plastic dinosaur flew, tail over snout. "Take that you poisonous bunch-back'd toad!" Conner scooped up a bottle of bubbles that had floated out of the toy basket and brandished it at the rampaging squirrel.

Instead of retreating, Rasputin sprang for Phooey. The wicked beast landed right between Phooey's ears and hung on tight.

Their big pup turned inside out. She slammed past the boys and bounded down the hall. She cried and bucked, smashing into the walls as she went.

"Back to the kitchen!" Conner shouted. He scooped something off the floor before Marcus ran over to help push him back down the hallway through the soaked carpet.

It was easy to know where their pup was headed since a cacophony of yowls and squeaks echoed back toward them.

The boys stopped at the door and peered into the kitchen.

Phooey yelped and bounded in a circle, leaving huge, soggy prints on the linoleum. Her tail whapped the side of the burning garbage can. The garbage can tipped, spilling burning trash across the linoleum and toward all the things Rasputin had dragged off the counters.

First, the empty flour sack caught. Then the recycling began to pop and crackle. Finally, Mom's basket of wallpaper samples burst into flame.

Marcus dashed forward, picking up the soaked towel he'd dropped.

Conner rolled so fast his chair skidded as he made a sharp turn. He brandished his soaked shirt in one hand and a wad of wet sponges from the bathroom in the other.

But the flood oozing up behind them was faster.

The river of water from the hallway caught up to Phooey, making her yelp and dance away. It washed across the kitchen, dousing the flames and filling the tipped garbage can with a swirl of damp ashes and debris.

Marcus paused to suck in a couple of deep breaths. OK, it was going to be OK. The fire was definitely out now. There was a flood, but at least the fire was out.

The squirrel chose that moment to make a break for it. He scampered down Phooey's back then launched off her rump with a graceful leap.

Phooey gave an almost squirrel-like squeak, herself. If King Kong had been a squirrel, he would have sounded just like her.

Everything had descended into chaos—again. Marcus had tried to trust God, but did it help? No. After Chaos arrived, it had invited all of its buddies over to play. Calamity, Destruction, and Obstreperous Behavior. Then Chaos and its buddies brought their pets: Boisterous Bunny, Frantic Feline, and Demolition Dino. Chaos to the 10th power and multiplied by pi. Marcus couldn't imagine a less peaceful scenario than what he beheld in wheelchair-safe house #4.

In the middle of it all, Conner called out to their trembling puppy.

Marcus blinked. She'd spent the last few days not listening, not hearing, not obeying. Why did his brother think that she would listen now?

Phooey's head snapped up. She looked around.

"Phooey Kerflooey! Here, girl. Come here!"

Phooey's drooping ears twitched, her slumping tail gave a tentative swish, and her eyes scanned the destruction until they locked onto Conner's.

Then Phooey did the craziest thing yet.

She bolted. Not away, but straight for Conner and his chair.

Phooey charged across the floor, took a flying leap, and landed right in Conner's lap with a splat. She pressed her soggy forehead into Conner's chest and shuddered. Their poor girl. She was so scared she'd even braved the wheelchair to find comfort.

Then something amazing happened. Her shaking stopped. Phooey eased away from Conner's chest and looked up into his eyes. Despite the chaos that filled the room, their scaredy pup's tongue lolled out the side of her mouth in a doggy grin and her fat tail started wagging.

You will keep in perfect peace . . . all whose thoughts are fixed on you.

There it was again. Not way back in Bible times with David and Goliath. Nope, it was right in front of them, bold and powerful and impossible.

Perfect peace.

Nothing around Phooey was perfect, nothing at all. But in the arms of her boy, looking up into his face, surrounded by chaos . . . Phooey Kerflooey had found perfect peace.

Marcus's chest tightened. Could peace have been his, all this time, if he'd just turned his eyes away from the chaos and focused on his Master?

You will keep in perfect peace . . . all whose thoughts are fixed on you.

He didn't have to train Phooey to be perfect. Didn't have to make Conner perfect. He didn't have to be perfect, not at all. Perfect peace could be his. Not just David's or Phooey's, but Marcus's, too.

Phooey Kerflooey

Phooey pressed her back against Conner's chest and settled into his lap with a sneeze and a single low growl.

Conner beamed up at Marcus, then turned his attention to their soggy dog. "You're such a brave girl, jumping all the way up here. I bet you could play basketball with hops like that!"

While his brother accepted face slurps and ear licks from Phooey, Marcus ran to turn off the water in the bathroom.

After finding the small shut-off valve under the sink, Marcus shone his flashlight down the hall. There, now if they could gather a bunch of towels and sop up all this water . . . It was a whole lot of water. So much water!

How many towels did they own? Would every single towel and washcloth and roll of paper towels be enough? Which would be worse, leaving some of the water or using the blankets from their beds to help clean up the mess? Mom and Dad were due home before bedtime.

The scuttle of small, clawed feet on the knickknack shelves that ran the length of the hallway just below the ceiling shook Marcus out of his thoughts. He looked up the hall, toward his parents' bedroom.

There, darting toward him with a confident flick of his tail, was Rasputin.

The sight froze Marcus where he stood.

The squirrel leapt off the knickknack shelf. He carried something in his mouth. A small black bag with fancy gold lettering that curved beneath the image of a single shimmering rose. The Gilded Blossom.

Mom's ring!

Marcus clutched the doorknob for balance as the furry tyrant chittered and scampered away, dragging the jewelry bag behind him.

That ratty squirrel was not going to ruin Mom's birthday on top of everything else!

Marcus broke into a run. What on earth was wrong with that horrible rodent? The paintballs at least looked like nuts. But jewelry? Now the furry wretch was just being mean.

Conner met him by the remains of the garbage can. "Did you see what that clod of wayward marl just made off with? I swear, if he gives one more flick of that fluffy tail, I'll . . . " Apparently, Conner's feelings were much too violent to voice near the tender ears of their puppy. Phooey looked up at Marcus's brother expectantly, her ears perked and head cocked to the side. Conner simply made some very enthusiastic choking motions in the air and glared.

Rasputin was frolicking from counter to counter, knocking over plastic cups and tramping through the ruined contents of a box of dry breakfast porridge. He dragged the jewelry bag through the entire mess.

Conner surged forward.

The squirrel bolted.

Marcus jumped to cut off his retreat and the furry marauder skittered sideways and then up, running across Mom's hanging flower pots as though they formed a squirrel highway.

The boys zipped and zoomed across the soggy room, Conner gripping a terrified Phooey in his lap. Marcus sprinted, slipped, and tumbled. Conner rolled and skidded. Phooey cowered and whined.

Rasputin was unstoppable.

After several exhausting minutes, they flopped in the corner by the blackened garbage can to get their breaths. Marcus wheezed and Conner, who wasn't quite as tired, had to apologize several times to Phooey, who dug her paws into this lap in fear. He offered her a treat out of the special bag hanging on the back of his chair.

Rasputin chittered his triumph.

Phooey flinched. She buried her snout under Conner's shirt and burrowed until she lay curled up against his chest. His shirt bulged out like a huge Santa belly.

Conner patted his puppy belly and smiled. "She's a great dog, Marcus. I don't want a Scottie. Thanks for picking Phooey. She's perfect."

Perfect?

Marcus glanced left and then right. Destroyed house, check. Rampaging squirrel, check. Lost jewelry, check. He looked back at his brother and the tender smile on Conner's face. A puppy who was brave enough to sit in Conner's chair for pets and snuggles, check.

Phooey Kerflooey

OK, so the Squirrel of the Apocalypse might have totally conquered the house, but Phooey had won over Conner. That's what Mom had wanted all along, right? Would a Scottie have done any better? Marcus wondered if Mom would notice the kitchen and the bathroom and the water in the hall and the blackened garbage can and her showroom and . . . everything.

Conner stroked Phooey's ears when she poked her nose out of his shirt collar to give him one more slurp. "You know, girl. I saved something for you." He whispered in Phooey's ear, loud enough for Marcus to hear, "Marcus threw your ballerina away, but I know what you like." Conner shot Marcus a mischievous grin and gave Phooey a gentle squeeze. "Just remember who loves you best. OK, Phooey Bear?"

From the hanging bag under his chair, Conner pulled out the TP doll with the pink crocheted skirt and the scary eyelashes.

Marcus's mouth dropped open, incredulous "Hey, I wasn't the one who traded Phooey's doll for that ridiculous ferret guy."

Conner shot him a grin. "Touché."

"How do you even know that word?"

"Cartoons, of course." Slowly, as though he were knighting a faithful servant of the crown, Conner clipped a bow above Phooey's ear and smoothed down her soft fur.

Phooey tipped her head to the side, gazing up at Conner with undisguised adoration. Then Conner gave her a kiss on the nose and held out the TP doll.

Phooey's tail thumped once, twice, then became a blur of wild wags. She wriggled out of Conner's shirt and seized the doll in her jaws.

Rasputin gave another arrogant trill.

This time, Phooey didn't flinch. She shook her doll like it was an attacking rat and stared back at the squirrel. A fierce gleam took over her sad brown eyes and Marcus heard a low rumble deep in her chest.

With a commanding yip that almost made her drop the doll, Phooey launched off Conner's lap and tore after the squirrel.

Rasputin didn't know where to run first. He skittered and scattered. Ran up cabinets and across the dried garlic hanging from the ceiling.

Phooey was relentless. She bounded right behind, snarling around the doll baby in her jaws and thundering like an avalanche of adorableness.

She cornered him in the back of the room, and then Rasputin turned mean. He nipped her tender snout with those sharp rodent teeth and scratched with his fierce, and tiny claws.

Phooey flinched back and Rasputin made a scamper for freedom, dodging toward her big paws where he could dart under her belly and be gone in an instant.

Right as the evil squirrel was about to get away, Marcus shouted out the command they'd been working on all weekend. The one Phooey had yet to get right.

"Sit!"

Without hesitation, Phooey sat, pinning the squirrel to the floor with her big furry bottom.

Phooey Kerflooey had saved her boys, and the day, and their mom's birthday ring . . . if not the house.

CHAPTER NINETEEN
Puppy Snuggles and an Epic Amount of Cleaning

Marcus got his brother settled in their fort and then went over his list of family-room campout items.

Tent made from the futon, old coffee table, and their only dry quilt—check.

The few squirrel-free snacks left in the house: a jar of green olives, a can of French-fried onions, and that jar of pepperoncinis—check.

The six-pack of juice boxes that Rasputin hadn't found—check.

Reading material (written by himself with illustrations by Conner) and flashlights—check, check.

Cleaning the house had taken forever, even after they'd found the big cotton mop and mop-squeezer bucket in the garage. Aunt Stella still hadn't returned. So Marcus had let go of his pride and called Nia.

She'd been happy to help, especially after the power came back on. The tree in her yard had fallen and it was either pick up tree rubble at her own house or squirrel rubble with the boys. All three of them did quite a bit of both. Dealing with tree rubble almost felt like a vacation after all their squirrel battles. He definitely should have asked her sooner, but they'd still gotten tons done before she had to go. While all the fans they could find were blowing on the hall carpet, the boys decided to camp out in the family room.

They'd used all the blankets and sheets to construct a dam at the entrance to the living room, saving Mom's favorite carpet from the worst of the flash flooding—if not the drink mix, crushed croutons, and baking soda. Marcus had used the mop while Nia pushed the mountain of fabric all over the rest of the house, sopping up the small lake that Rasputin and Phooey had worked so hard to create.

Marcus had swept.

Conner had used the shop vac on the noodles, croutons, and scattered spit peas.

Nia had vacuumed drink mix out of the carpet.

Marcus wiped the back of the counters.

Conner wiped the front of the counters.

Nia had thrown away the burnt wallpaper samples and put dry bows in Phooey's fur.

Nia was home now, and both boys sagged with exhaustion. There wasn't anywhere else to sleep besides their new fort. All the beds were bare, as well as the closets.

Conner was propped up on pillows in the back of the fort, popping green olives in his mouth and grimacing at the sour flavor while he cuddled Phooey. Marcus crawled in to join them.

He'd written a fairytale for Phooey and Conner had drawn the pictures. It was good to finally create another improbable episode of mayhem together. The comic book kind, nothing real or involving squirrels!

Marcus leaned back against his pillow while Conner held up their newly finished story for Phooey to see. It was the story of Cinderella. Or at least something vaguely like Cinderella.

Marcus launched into the tale, doing all the voices and pausing for Phooey to sniff each new page. She seemed to approve of both the plot line and the illustrations, although Conner was going to have to redraw the pages that showed the food at the ball. Phooey had sniffed them very thoroughly.

"And Cinderfluffums wagged her tail and galloped around the ball room, snorking down snacks and planting her big paws in the middle of fancy ball gowns and incredibly tidy suits so that she could slurp the faces of everyone who looked like they needed cheering up. But at the stroke of midnight, Cinderfluffums gave a single howl and galloped into the night.

"Then the handsome prince realized that he didn't need a wife—he needed a dog. A big dog. A fluffy dog. A dog who could drink out of the punch bowl without any help from the butler."

Conner grinned and snuggled Phooey closer. She lay her head on her paws and seemed to hang on every word.

"And so, the prince sent his faithful servants out into the land, each holding a clump of dog hair that Cinderfluffums had left at the ball. There was plenty of hair for all the searchers, as Cinderfluffums had shed generously. Eventually one of the snooty footmen came to the rundown mansion where Cinderfluffums was living in servitude. As the poor dog was unhooked from her vegetable cart and shoved into the garden shed where she would spend the night in lonely exile with no one to slurp, a sound made her prick her ears.

"The snooty footman read the scroll that the prince had stapled to the clump of dog fur: 'Cinderfluffums! Here, girl!'

"Cinderfluffums was filled with joy."

Phooey thumped her tail against the tent, making the whole structure shudder.

"She burst out of her prison and leapt into the arms of the snooty footman. He fell over backwards and landed in a mud puddle, but that was all right because Cinderfluffums was there to lick him clean.

"Her former owner was banned from ever owning a dog again and forced to house all the stray cats in the city. Cinderfluffums was given 109 couches to lounge upon, 32 huge punchbowls to drink from, and one mischievous prince . . . " Marcus looked up at Conner. "Make that *two* mischievous princes to gallop around the palace with. They lived happily ever after, and dog hair sweaters became the height of fashion. Cinderfluffums even saved the crown jewels with her extravagant shedding. While other kingdoms had to sell all of their costliest gems in order to import wagonloads of dog hair to clothe their royalty, Cinderfluffums shed enough so that the entire royal family had a dog-hair sweater for every day of the week!"

Phooey was overcome with wagging and launched herself at Conner, smashing him back into his pillows as she planted her paws on his chest and thoroughly washed his ears.

Then she tackled Marcus as well. After he'd been duly cleansed, Marcus wriggled out from under her enthusiastic attack. He smoothed the soft fur on top of her head and gave their pup a gentle hug.

Marcus glanced at his brother. Conner was beaming. Sure, Phooey wasn't what they'd expected, but she was just what they needed. A dog to snuggle and train and tell stories to. A dog who would inspire them to clean the house more thoroughly than they ever thought was humanly possible. A dog to chase away mean squirrels and who loved them best, out of all the people in the world.

Marcus didn't know if God had planned for him to bring home Phooey, or if she was simply a wonderful accident. It didn't matter, though. Either way, God had brought them a tiny slice of perfect peace, even in the middle of their squirrel apocalypse, regardless of all the wrecked plans . . . and carpeting.

Rasputin gave an angry *cheep* from inside the old birdcage where Marcus had trapped him. Hopefully Dad could help them release him safely—somewhere far, *far* away.

Phooey let a low, rumbling growl fill her chest and the squirrel stopped his rude talk.

The front door creaked open and footsteps came down the hall. "Oh, my goodness. You boys mopped. A lot. Why are all these fans running?" Mom's face peered into their tent and a soft look stole over her features. Then her gentle smile was replaced by a frown. "You're getting attached, aren't you? This puppy isn't even the right breed. I made a terrible mistake, boys. We have to take her back."

Marcus met Mom's gaze. He thought of the list in his notebook. *Perils of Keeping Phooey: 1) Too much fur. 2) Strings of dog slobber. 3) Must live with TP doll and her terrifying eyelashes. 4) Too much howling and fearful peeing. 5) Too many warm snuggles. 6) The mind-numbing power of puppy eyes. 7) Avalanche of wet kisses and snurffles. 8) Lots of hard work.* Maybe some things are worth lots of hard work.

Marcus started to explain, but Conner beat him to it.

"Phooey's our girl, Mom. She's big and fluffy and brave and pretty. She rescued your super-expensive birthday present and she even saved us from a terrible death by squirrel attack." Conner jabbed at the birdcage, which gave an angry trill and rattled threateningly. Marcus saw that there were tears in his brother's eyes as he pulled Phooey close and gave her a fierce squeeze.

"What about those four little kids who wanted to buy Phooey?"

Marcus saw that Conner was in no shape to reply. He wouldn't want Mom to hear the tears in his voice. "They can get their own puppy, Mom," Marcus said. "Phooey wants us and we want her."

Dad poked his head in beside Mom. "Phooey, huh?" He reached out to ruffle Phooey's ears. She leaned into his hand with a contented grumble. "Speaking of that super-expensive birthday present, do you think Phooey wants to do the honors, boys?" Dad held up the black bag with the shiny gold lettering. Phooey pricked up her ears.

Marcus lunged for the fancy bag before Phooey got any ideas. "Better let us, Dad. Phooey might eat it."

Dad's eyebrows shot up at that, but he didn't ask any questions.

Marcus handed the gift to Conner, who hummed dramatically, waved the bag in the air, and then held it out to Mom with a "Bum, bum, bum . . . ta-da!"

Mom's eyes were all misty as she snapped open the black ring box. "Oh, my!" She put a hand to her heart and admired each stone, turning the box this way and that so the light sparkled off the polished gold. Phooey leaned closer, clearly admiring the shiny piece of jewelry.

"She almost looks like she wants to see it." Mom held the velvet box out toward the pup. Marcus and Conner squeezed Phooey tight, lest their puppy princess snork down Mom's new ring . . . again.

"Phooey loves pretty things, Mom." Marcus added. "I got a female puppy so you would have another girl around the house. She loves bows in her fur, Princess music, and her doll baby. You're always saying that everything around here is either camo, navy blue, or navy-blue camo and you could use a, Marcus made quote marks in the air with his fingers, "'touch of pink.' Phooey can be our touch of pink."

Marcus held up the somewhat-chewed TP doll as evidence when his Mom gave Phooey a skeptical look.

"And you boys are certain that this is the puppy you want? I know she isn't what any of us expected."

"She's perfect, Mom," Conner said, getting a big slurp across the face for his efforts.

Marcus sent up a silent prayer. They couldn't lose Phooey, not after all they'd been through. His stomach ached at the thought.

"Well . . . " Mom hesitated as she eyed the giant puppy. Then she reached out tentatively and buried her fingers in the pup's soft, black fur. "The Newfie breeder says she'll require weekly grooming and lots of training. I noticed quite a few broken things in the living room. You boys have to help me fix everything she messes up while she's learning."

"Of course," Marcus replied. He blew out the breath he'd been holding and it felt as though his heart had started beating again after sitting frozen in his chest, waiting for Mom's answer.

She held up a finger for them to stop. "And I want five new moth paintings." She glanced at their dad meaningfully and he nodded, hiding a smile.

Dad glanced around, then shook his head. "All I can say is that it's a good thing we sprung for the pricier house insurance."

Conner smiled. "We're up for the hard work. She already knows 'sit' and we gave her a bath, too. Several baths, actually. And look, feeding her will be super-easy." Conner lifted his walkie-talkie. "You're on!"

The whole family waited a moment and then the back door burst open. As Dad and Mom turned toward the sound, Nia charged into the room and pointed at her brand-new Rube Goldberg machine. "This is the answer to all your dog-feeding anguish, folks. Just watch and learn."

Nia lit the candle and turned on a little fan that she'd used instead of Phooey's wagging tail.

The tiny fan pushed a wooden marble out of its resting place and into the spiral slide. The marble hit the row of dominoes at the bottom. The dominoes smashed the first toy car down the ramp. The car shook the cardboard tube, knocking off the matchbox full of glass marbles. The marbles showered into the mouth of the funnel, traveled down the paper towel tube, and finally tumbled against the alien car with the lit candle on top. The car rolled under the string. The small flame ate through the string, which broke, sending a big plastic cup full of dog food tipping over and into Phooey's dish.

"Oh, wow. You weren't kidding, Nia. This machine works beautifully." Mom's expression grew thoughtful and then she noticed the homemade book in Conner's lap. "Did you guys write another comic?"

Both Marcus and Conner nodded.

"Of course they did," Nia said. "They've been in a creative—but totally calm—frenzy for like twenty whole minutes." Her phone chimed. "Welp, better go. Looks like Nefurious got out of his three-piece suit." Their neighbor darted out the door, leaving a trail of sparkles, ear bows, and one tasty dog cookie behind.

Phooey immediately took care of that lonely cookie, free of charge.

As Mom glanced through the comic, her face lit up with the brightest smile Marcus had seen in over a year. She gave Phooey a pat and their pup's tail thumped against the floor. "She looks like a real snuggler, and I love the bow! Nicely done, boys."

Rasputin gave another angry chirp and Mom jumped.

"Wait till you hear how she caught that awful squirrel." Conner pointed to the bird cage as Phooey gave a demonstration of her fierce growling.

Marcus pulled their pup into his lap. Mom had been correct. He had been able to make the choice. He had chosen the perfect puppy for them.

"Oh, I just got a text from the Newfie breeder, boys. That family picked out a pup named Dice."

Marcus scratched Phooey's belly. Not that he would have ever given up Phooey, but he was glad for the other family. Glad that they'd found their perfect puppy, too.

The door creaked again. Phooey grabbed up her doll baby and let loose a fierce bark. Marcus grinned. She was getting so brave.

"Gracious gophers!" Aunt Stella shouted down the hall. "I've finally got pizza, boys. Did anything interesting happen while I was gone?"

EPILOGUE
One month later...

The moving truck rattled up a twisty mountain road. Dad was now Maintenance Director for Camp Castle Pine and Nia's dad had gotten the job of Program Director. Basically, Nia's dad would run all the fun games and their dad would fix all the stuff that everyone broke. Dad had already been doing that job with Conner, anyway.

Marcus grinned at Conner as Phooey's ears flattened and she burrowed into his armpit. Marcus cuddled her close. Well, as much of her as would fit on his lap. Her back half was plopped onto Conner's lap. Dad had helped Conner into the cab of the moving truck to sit between them for the ride to his new job and their new home.

Conner patted her rump.

Phooey gave a tentative wag.

"You don't fit, girl. Just enjoy the ride. Sniff that mountain breeze. Dream of chasing a whole forest full of squirrels."

Phooey poked her nose out of Marcus's armpit for an instant, as if looking for this fabled "mountain breeze." She'd already gained ten pounds since they got her. Phooey was definitely not pocket-sized.

Marcus unrolled the window and stuck his head into the sunshine. Towering ponderosa pines and shaggy firs lined the remote gravel road. Clumps of razor grass and spring wildflowers carpeted the forest floor. The air was scented with the sweet nectar of blossoms, drifting pine pollen, and the sharp smell of tree sap warming in the sun.

As the moving truck chugged higher and higher into the mountains, the wind grew crisp and wild. It tossed Marcus's hair back from his face and made his cheeks tingle with cold, even as the bright sun warmed them.

Phooey gave a tentative sniff and began to wag. "See, girl. This is where it's at." She eyed Marcus and then the open window. Her ears went from a worried tilt to pricked.

He gave an exaggerated sniff and huge sigh of contentment. "Think of all the smells I'm sniffing, Phooey. And my nose isn't half as good as yours. What this window needs is a real nose to sniff out it. If only there was someone with such a nose to sniff these beautiful smells."

The furry lump bounded out from under Marcus's arm, tripped over the notebook on his lap, then plopped her big front paws on the armrest and poked her head out the window.

Marcus cuddled her close as she sniffed busily, clearly cataloging every new scent and putting a few things into her "must roll in later" file.

When they finally crested the hill and chugged around the last corner, a mountain meadow came into view. A sea of tall, waving grasses and scattered wildflowers was ringed by a crescent of log buildings.

Camp Castle Pine.

Barely visible in the distance, a massive twisting tree towered above the others. It grew at the edge of a cliff and looked down on the frigid waters of a mountain lake. The twin trunks of ancient ponderosa pines were twined together, looking almost like some kind of fortress. This monster of a tree had given the camp its name.

Right before they pulled up to the main lodge, Dad steered the moving van down a tiny dirt road that meandered off into the thick trees. They bumped along for maybe a mile before a sprawling ranch house made of logs appeared.

A full, wrap-around porch circled the structure, complete with a swing in front of huge picture windows. A ramp sloped upward alongside a set of rough-cut log steps and log railing. A small archery range sat to the left of the house. Near the archery range, a wooden cabinet was nailed to twin firs and presumably held bows and arrows.

Tucked into the woods just past the house stood a tree fort. It was unlike any fort Marcus had ever seen. When he shot Conner a look, a gigantic smile lit up his brother's face.

The truck rumbled to a stop.

Situated between the trunks of three mighty pines, the first level of the tree fort was a wide platform about six feet off the ground. It had a rustic log railing, hand-crafted log chairs, and a locking equipment cabinet that just might be squirrel-proof. The platform was accessible by a sloping ramp.

Another ramp, complete with log railings and a pulley system for helping heave a wheelchair up the steeper slope, led up to a second-story platform that encircled the left-most tree. Finally, a third ramp sloped up to the tree on the far right, where a crow's nest-style platform circled its trunk high above the ground.

Past the log railing on that highest perch, Marcus could just see a series of heavy nylon straps hanging from the roof. They were clustered near a wooden captain's chair with a drink holder on one arm and a telescope on the other. Conner would be able to hoist himself out of his wheelchair to sit in the captain's seat.

Marcus looked closer. There were handy nylon straps all over the tree fort. Plus, a canvas hammock hung between two of the trunks on the first level. A bookshelf and small cabinet were situated by the hammock, which swung gently in the light breeze. A perfect nook for him.

Marcus jumped out of the truck and lowered Phooey to the carpet of pine needles on the ground. She pranced in a circle, lifting her paws high and barking at the strangeness of the forest floor. But after a moment, some amazing mountain smell must have distracted her. She set off, tail wagging out a happy rhythm.

Dad helped Conner out of the truck and settled him into a new wheelchair. Instead of tiny front wheels, this one was built more like a giant tricycle. It had three huge wheels. They were thick and knobby, clearly built for rough terrain. Conner pumped a fist in the air and spun the chair toward the tree fort.

A shrill chittering drew Marcus's attention back to the moving truck.

Rasputin hung upside down from the undercarriage. He flicked an angry tail and darted along the side of the truck, heading toward the open back end where all their boxes waited in tempting stacks.

"Rasputin, no!" Marcus ran toward the truck, hoping to head the squirrel off before he could burrow into their things and wreak further destruction.

But Phooey beat him to it.

With a fierce woof, Phooey bounded ahead, tail wagging in a circle to keep her balance. She tore after Rasputin, barking and bouncing, her ears flapping with every leap.

The squirrel turned. He darted across the forest floor in a flash and dashed up into the branches of a bristly fir.

Marcus watched Rasputin leap from branch to branch. Graceful as an Olympic gymnast, the lithe animal took to the trees with a beautiful strength that made something in Marcus's chest swell with joy. Rasputin was where he belonged.

Phooey pranced over and sat at Marcus's feet, wagging. "You're such a good girl." Marcus ruffled her ears and bent to let her slurp his face. "That poor squirrel didn't know about the trees, but you helped him out. Chased him all the way home."

They walked to the moving van and Marcus grabbed a small box that he'd tucked in last. He opened the lid and pulled out a hammer and handful of nails. Then he carried the box up to their new house. He set it down on the porch and pulled out a sign. Marcus stood on a chair and pounded a single nail into the wood above the front door. He hung up the sign then hopped down and looked up at his handiwork.

You will keep in perfect peace . . . all whose thoughts are fixed on you. —Isaiah 26:3

He walked back to the truck and stood beside Dad as he unloaded. "What should I carry in first?"

Dad slowly straightened his back. He looked down at Marcus and smiled. "I could use you boys' help in about thirty minutes when Mom gets here. But I'm pretty sure that tree fort should be broken in first."

Marcus stepped into his dad's hug, grabbed the book he was reading, and ran to the tree fort.

Right as he started up the first ramp, a crash issued from the forest. Birds took flight in an explosion of winged panic. Pounding footsteps, and then Nia appeared. There, hidden in the trees, was the small path that wound between their houses.

Nefurious growled softly from where he'd been slung over Nia's shoulder, and Porky and Tater Tot trilled from the mesh carrier she held in her other hand.

"You found the fort!" Nia shouted up toward his brother. Then she tied the cat's leash to the guinea pig carrier, plopped them on the grass, and did a cartwheel. She gave Marcus a high five, retrieved her critters, and then pounded up the ramp toward Conner.

Marcus laughed and followed. Phooey bounded at his heels. She gave a happy bark and galloped up the ramp, all on her own.

Marcus jogged after her. They'd taught their new puppy a lot. She sure wouldn't have done that a month ago. He looked up at Conner who was sitting in the captain's chair and Nia who was darting around the crow's nest, showing a hissing Nefurious all of the available trees for climbing. Not that the overweight feline was likely to do so, but clearly Nia believed in him.

Marcus smiled and settled into the hammock, book in hand, without writing a single danger down in his little notebook. Phooey had taught him a whole lot, too. He reached down and scooped her into his lap. Then pulled her dolly out of his back pocket.

Her eyes grew wide with the swaying motion. But after a moment she gripped her doll in her jaws, stretched out on his chest and closed her eyes, tail thumping.

He stroked her soft fur. They'd finally found their perfect peace. Sure, their world was still plenty chaotic and none of them was perfect, but there could still be perfect peace. God had turned the impossible into something real.

He closed his eyes, listening to the sounds. Above, his brother wheeling his chair up and down the ramps. Nia telling her guinea pigs about all the tasty grasses in the meadow. Mom talking to Dad while checking off boxes on her list and Dad laughing. Wind rustling the treetops and birdsong filling the stillness. Finally, the soft *swish, swish, swish* of Phooey's tail wagging against the hammock. Marcus hugged their puppy tight.

Phooey slurped his cheek and then proceeded to wash his ears.

Marcus opened up his book and nudged the hammock into motion. Phooey curled into a ball in his lap and Rasputin joined another squirrel for a game of tag in the branches far, far above.

For just a moment, everything was perfect. Marcus stroked Phooey's fur and whispered a prayer of thanks. Because of Phooey Kerflooey, he knew that even when perfection faded and the chaos returned, he could still have perfect peace.

The End

CONNER'S RECIPE FOR PUPPY BIRTHDAY CAKE

Ingredients

1 to 3 cans of tuna fish, depending on the size of your dog.

1 can of Vienna sausages

6 slices of pepperoni

2 Tablespoons of bacon bits

1 birthday candle

Directions

Open the cans of tuna with a can opener. Be careful of the sharp edges. Drain out the juices. Dump the tuna into a mound in the center of a plate.

Open the can of Vienna sausages. Place each

sausage in an upright position around the mound of tuna like the fancy columns in an ancient Greek building.

Place the slices of pepperoni between the Vienna sausages.

Sprinkle the cake with bacon bits. Place the candle in the center of your cake.

Get your parents to help you light the candle.

Sing "Happy Birthday" to your puppy. Make sure that he or she does not burn a nose trying to blow out the candle. You will probably have to blow it out yourself.

Set the cake on the floor and release your puppy!

Get lots of pictures of your pup tearing into this meaty cake.

UNWANTED, UNEXPECTED, A WHISPER, A GIFT

A True Story

I Kings 19:11-13a

"'Go out and stand before me on the mountain,' the LORD told him. And as Elijah stood there, the LORD passed by, and a mighty windstorm hit the mountain. It was such a terrible blast that the rocks were torn loose, but the LORD was not in the wind. After the wind there was an earthquake, but the LORD was not in the earthquake. And after the earthquake there was a fire, but the LORD was not in the fire. And after the fire there was the sound of a gentle whisper. When Elijah heard it, he wrapped his face in his cloak and went out and stood at the entrance of the cave." NLT

"I'm not fond of cats." This was always my husband's (Scruffy) typical answer when anyone asked why we didn't have a cat, had never had a cat, not even once during our 23-year-marriage. This was an incredible understatement.

But Scruff didn't really hate cats.

What he hated was a childhood filled with cigarette smoke, tension, cutting manipulation, and the pervasive scent of cat urine. What he hated was going to school where there was the chance of kindness, a smile, maybe friendship . . . only to have a kid wrinkle their nose at how he smelled. It doesn't matter how carefully you launder your clothes, if the house is full of smoke and cats.

Over the years, as God brought healing and joy and new life, Scruff softened a bit toward cats, until everything changed on a frosty morning in November.

Someone dumped a half-grown kitten on the mountain meadow where we live. Our neighbor was getting the mail (yes, our mailbox is two miles away from our house and so is theirs) and saw a wet, skinny, orange tabby shivering underneath a hunter's pickup truck. The hunter said he had no idea where she'd come from and he didn't want her.

Now, anyone who has approached a stray cat knows that they are a skittish bunch.

Our neighbor didn't have time to chase a hissing, scratching creature around the forest. "I'll just try once," he told himself as he bent and peered into her hiding place. She came right to him.

Phooey Kerflooey

We lost our beloved Newfoundland dog, Princess Leia Freyja, this year and are on a list for a puppy. So when our neighbor texted, asking if anyone had lost a female tabby, I was shocked at my husband's reply.

"Let us know if you need help homing it. We've been considering getting one."

What? Was this really my husband? We had not been considering getting one. What had been happening was that every single cat lover in our lives had been sending Scruff photos of adorable kittens in need for the past twenty years and he'd been consistently telling them, "Absolutely not!"

Long story short, we now have a cat.

I wanted to name her Persnickety, because it is the ideal cat name. Scruff wanted to name her Whisper, because despite her harsh start in life, alone and wet on a frosty morning huddled under a stranger's truck, she is an incredibly gentle cat with the softest voice. A gentle whisper.

Like how God appears to us as we press on through a life that can be so incredibly hard. He doesn't come like a blast of dynamite, a tornado of power, a world-shattering earthquake (although He can and occasionally, He has). More often, He steps into the darkness of our world with a quiet whisper that changes everything.

AND AFTER THE FIRE CAME A GENTLE WHISPER. (I KINGS 19:12B)

Phooey Kerflooey

Whisper was unloved, unwanted, abandoned on a lonely morning to the cold of a forest full of predators. Have you ever lived that moment? I have. The quiet despair of a strange place, the biting cold of abandonment, the danger, the vast loneliness.

She is clearly not a feral cat. Whisper doesn't have the harsh independence of those tough and cagy felines that make their own way in the world.

Whisper Persnickety rushes to join me whenever I get out of bed to use the bathroom. She follows me around the house with a quiet mew and bumps against my legs to cuddle and trip me up. When I settle into my little loft office to write, she curls up against my feet and snoozes until I put the final word to the page. When I read in front of the fire, she curls up on my lap and dozes. At night, as soon as Scruff crawls into bed she hops up with a soft meow and curls herself against his side.

"I can't believe someone didn't want this cat," Scruffy told me last night.

The man who felt the heartache of an unhappy childhood every time he saw a cat. This is the man who said that. She has been such a gift as we grieve the loss of our Leia, as we wait on that puppy list, as we miss the presence of a warm fuzzy in our lives. As we missed something we'd never had, a warm cat curled up next to us in bed, purring softly.

Phooey Kerflooey

Whisper is a gentle, loving cat with good manners and a peaceful presence.

Someone didn't want her.

If you feel unwanted, today, I want you to stop a moment and listen closely.

Is our Whisper any less valuable because someone didn't want her? Is she less gentle, less loving, less beautiful because she was found abandoned at the end of a road? Is she less a gift because she was unexpected? Isn't she the whisper of God's voice come into our lives when we were hurting? Yes, yes she is and you can be, too.

You are valuable.

You are a gift.

You can be the gentle whisper of a powerful God into the lives of hurting people.

Are there people who don't want you?

It doesn't matter.

There is one who does.

There is one who loves you deeply, who seeks you when you find yourself lost and alone, who rescues.

Lost sheep.

Lost kittens.

Lost people.

He calls you to follow, to love like He loves.

For just like Jesus . . .

You, little one, you are a whisper of hope.

Luke 19:10

"For the Son of Man came to seek and save those who are lost." NLT

Luke 15:3-6

"So Jesus told them this story:

'If a man has a hundred sheep and one of them gets lost, what will he do? Won't he leave the ninety-nine others in the wilderness and go to search for the one that is lost until he finds it? And when he has found it, he will joyfully carry it home on his shoulders. When he arrives, he will call together his friends and neighbors, saying, 'Rejoice with me because I have found my lost sheep.'" NLT

Phooey Kerflooey

John 10:10-11

"The thief's purpose is to steal and kill and destroy. My purpose is to give them a rich and satisfying life. I am the good shepherd. The good shepherd sacrifices his life for the sheep." NLT

Psalm 23
"The LORD is my shepherd;
I have all that I need.

He lets me rest in green meadows;
he leads me beside peaceful streams.

He renews my strength.
He guides me along right paths,
bringing honor to his name.

Even when I walk
through the darkest valley,
I will not be afraid,
for you are close beside me.
Your rod and your staff
protect and comfort me.

You prepare a feast for me
in the presence of my enemies.
You honor me by anointing my head with oil.
My cup overflows with blessings.

Surely your goodness and unfailing love will pursue
me
all the days of my life,

and I will live in the house of the LORD forever." NLT

John 3:16-17

"'For God loved the world so much that he gave his one and only Son, so that everyone who believes in him will not perish but have eternal life. God sent his Son into the world not to judge the world, but to save the world through him.'" NLT

John 15:12 NLT

"This is my commandment: Love each other in the same way I have loved you."

ACKNOWLEDGEMENTS

Thank you to Janet Hohnhorst Reiff for letting me use the story of how she had to race her Newfoundland Dice to bed or he would take up the entire mattress. Also, that story of how Dice ate two huge meals while she and her sister were perusing a yard sale (two hamburgers, two fries, two coleslaws, two big desserts, all the condiments) and then was ready for dinner that night. That story was gold!

Thank you to Anna Ubel of the Newfoundland dog owner's forum for the fabulous tale of how your pup Belle dashed into the shower with you, bounced you off the wall, became tangled in the curtain, and then thundered off taking the shower curtain with her. So funny!

Thank you to our own pup, Princess Leia Freyja Wilks. Thank you for stealing giant jawbreakers, wanting ice in your water dish, being afraid to potty without an escort, raising your eyebrows to let us know someone left a book on "your" couch, for all your princess ways, and for all of the love and slobber that you gave to your three boys.

I want to thank my three amazing sons: Judah, Theo, and Brennan. Their penchant for adventures has kept our lives interesting and worthy of any number of weighty tomes full of laughter and mayhem. Also, they requested that I write stories inspired by their puppy, but were horrified that the boys in my story were not immediately thrilled that their pup was a giant princess! Don't worry, boys, they grow to love her princess ways. I realize that you are all too old to read this one now. . . but as C.S. Lewis said, ". . . some day you will be old enough to start reading fairy tales again."

Thank you to my camp director husband, Scruffy. Not only did you chase squirrels out of our house and save the day, but you consistently encouraged my dream of writing for years and years and years before I saw a cent of profit. You gave me encouragement, ideas, time to write, and even washed dishes at 1:00AM so that we're not buried! You truly are my hero.

A huge shout out to Jennifer Dyer, my amazing critique partner who saw so many different versions of this story that it's amazing she doesn't twitch with alarm every time she sees a shaggy dog or cheeping squirrel! Also, to my wonderful editor Devon Steele, for giving this story its final polish, thank you so much!

Hooray to my character artist Haley Kohler (hekohlerart) for bringing Marcus, Conner, Nia, Rasputin, and Phooey to life! Thank you, Lynette Bonner (IndieCoverDesign) for designing the beautiful cover.

Phooey Kerflooey

Much thanks to Brett Johnson and Nancy Bywater-Johnson, who work in special education at our local public schools. You showed me that there is no limit to the mayhem a child in a wheelchair can cause. Your stories about making adventures possible for campers of every ability were so inspiring. From horseback and kayak rides to swimming lessons and plunges from the diving board, you made sure that each child enjoyed every activity they wanted to, and that their chairs absolutely did not keep them out of the action!

Linda Howard, when you pulled me into a hug at that writers conference and told me that you loved my writing, that all your editors loved my writing, it filled me with just enough courage to keep going. Thank you.

And finally, thank you to my rescuer, Jesus Messiah. You made me with a passion for story and have given me strength for hard times, the ability to laugh and weep and press forward, and eyes to see every ridiculous thing that might brighten a dark day. You have both kept me close and given me wings. May every word, even the silly ones, bring honor to You.

I do **NOT** thank the various squirrels who have invaded our house or the camp where we work. No! I do not thank you for the holes chewed in the window screen so that you could break in. The nibbles left in our various food stuffs. I do not thank you for the angry chittering, the epic chases through the house, that dangerous fire started at Grandpa Del's when one of you chewed through a power tool cord, or the stinky brown pellets left on my pillow in revenge. I will never feed a squirrel again. If feeding bears is

Phooey Kerflooey

unwise, feeding squirrels is apocalyptic.

ABOUT THE AUTHOR

Kristen Joy Wilks was once a barefoot girl on horseback, galloping through the remote forests and hidden meadows surrounding a small Bible camp in the Cascade Mountains. She has carried a frog in her pocket, captained dubious watercraft made from old boards and inner tubes, and directed her horse through a herd of 200 elk against all good sense. Due to a brilliant scheme with her cousins, she has even been suspended by her feet over a pit filled with gardener snakes. Despite this experience, she returns to the mountains again and again.

Kristen is married to a camp director and has three mountain boys of her own. Their family is owned by a large and slobbery Newfoundland dog and a cat named Whisper Persnickety. **Kristen writes about the humor and grace found amidst the detritus of life.** She can be found at Camas Meadows Bible Camp snapping photos, **www.KristenJoyWilks.com**, or in an overstuffed chair at 4:00 AM writing a wide variety of implausible tales.

Phooey Kerflooey

FREE STUFF!

Be a part of the adventure by coloring your own Phooey, Rasputin, Marcus, Connor, or Nia! Scan below to get Kristen's free coloring pages below.

Which parts of the story are real?
Scan below to read about extreme wheelchair jumping
and Kristen's real-life stories of squirrel chases,
puppy mayhem, and that time one of her sons crashed
into a toilet and had to get stiches!

Or get the Phooey Kerflooey e-book for free by signing up for Kristen's Newsletter below. Her quarterly newsletter provides stories of mountain life, news about upcoming books, and tips for getting kiddos reading and outside into God's beautiful creation.

Phooey Kerflooey

Phooey Kerflooey

Phooey Kerflooey

Phooey Kerflooey

Phooey Kerflooey